THE MAGNIFICENT LIZZIE BROWN AND THE MYSTERIOUS PHANTOM

BY VICKI LOCKWOOD

COVER ILLUSTRATION BY STEPHANIE HANS

capstone
young readers

The Magnificent Lizzie Brown is published in the United States in 2015
by Capstone Young Readers,
A Capstone Imprint
1710 Roe Crest Drive
North Mankato, Minnesota 56003
www.capstoneyoungreaders.com

First published in 2014 by Curious Fox,
an imprint of Capstone Global Library Limited,
7 Pilgrim Street, London, EC4V 6LB
Registered company number: 6695582
www.curious-fox.com

Library of Congress Cataloging-in-Publication Data
Lockwood, Vicki, author.
  The magnificent Lizzie Brown and the mysterious phantom / by Vicki Lockwood ; illustrated
by Stephanie Hans.
     pages cm. -- (The magnificent Lizzie Brown)
  Summary: In nineteenth-century London Lizzie Brown wants nothing more than to escape
from the slums and her drunk, abusive father, so finding work and friends in a passing
circus seems like a dream come true — but when she starts to have visions she finds herself
confronting the mysterious phantom of London.

  ISBN 978-1-4342-7940-8 (library binding) -- ISBN 978-1-62370-069-0 (paper over board) -- ISBN
978-1-4342-7942-2 (pbk.) -- ISBN 978-1-4965-0099-1 (ebook PDF)

  1. Psychic ability--Juvenile fiction. 2. Circus--Juvenile fiction. 3. Criminals--Juvenile fiction. 4.
London (England)--History--19th century--Juvenile fiction. [1. Mystery and detective stories. 2.
Psychic ability--Fiction. 3. Circus--Fiction. 4. Criminals--Fiction. 5. London England)--History-
-19th century--Fiction. 6. Great Britain--History--19th century--Fiction.] I. Hans, Stephanie,
illustrator. II. Title.

  PZ7.L8192Mag 2014
  813.6--dc23

                                    2013050830

Cover illustration: Stephanie Hans
Designer: Kristi Carlson

Printed in China.
032014   008116WAIF14

With special thanks to
Kate Cary and Adrian Bott

CHAPTER 1

"Ain't you up yet, girl?" Pa snapped, jerking Lizzie awake with his iron grip.

"All right, all right!' Lizzie shook him off and kicked free of her ragged blanket. She swung her legs over the side of her rough wooden bed and stuck her feet into her boots.

The early light of dawn filtered through the rags pinned over the window. The cracked door to Lizzie's tiny bedroom was still swinging where Pa had barged through. He was carrying a package wrapped in tattered newspaper. For a foolish moment, Lizzie wondered if he'd been out to fetch her a present. Perhaps he'd brought something good to eat. That would be a nice change from yesterday's dry bread.

But then Pa slammed the package down on the table. Lizzie guessed from the clunk that it was a bottle of gin, and her heart sank.

"Are you drinkin' already?" Lizzie muttered.

"I'll need somethin' to keep me warm while I'm out there earnin' enough to keep you." Pa glared at her resentfully as he sat on the edge of the bed and began rolling up his pants. "Give me the soap and vinegar. I'm using the Scaldrum Dodge — need to fake some sores. Be quick, lazy-legs. I want to catch the rich folks on their way to work."

Lizzie jumped to her feet and grabbed the soap from its dish, then passed it to Pa. As she stood on tiptoes to reach the jar of vinegar above, she had to push aside the brightly colored paper she'd hidden behind the rafters the night before, safely out of sight. The money she'd earned doing laundry for Mrs. Buckle had been enough to buy all she needed to make paper flowers. A bouquet of handmade posies might earn enough to get a room of her own somewhere far, far away from here.

Lizzie lived in Rat's Castle, London's filthiest slum. It was thick with thieves and choked by stench. Houses leaned against each other, and the tiny alleys between them were no more than sewers. Dead ends, courts, and yards forked this way and that, with passages below and walkways above that felons could run through like vermin. To Lizzie it had always been home, but she found life there unbearable.

There were six children living in the room next to Lizzie and Pa's, along with a mother and grandmother. They were all crammed into two beds with only an oil lamp between them. Lizzie could hear them now, the baby wailing with hunger, the children squabbling, and the grandmother yelling at her daughter. Upstairs, men snored and grunted, sleeping off the drink that had them roaring most of the night.

Lizzie looked at the bright paper fluttering above her, whispering the promise of a new life, and smiled to herself.

"What you smirkin' at?" Pa broke into Lizzie's daydream, and she nearly dropped the vinegar. She knew that tone of voice. It was dangerous.

"Nothing, Pa." She slid the jar onto the table, but to her horror she saw that her streamers had caught his eye.

"What you want that nonsense for?" Pa began to rub soap thickly over his shins. "Wastin' good money."

"It ain't wasted, Pa," Lizzie argued. "I'm gonna make flowers to sell on Rotten Row."

"Lot of hard work." Pa's legs were streaked yellow with soap. "Why work when you can turn your hand to some useful beggin' or thievin'? Rich folks are there for us to steal from. I've spent enough time teaching you how to pinch a penny out of someone's pocket. You're twelve now, so you should be bringin' in money of yer own. A skinny, sickly looking girl like you will fetch plenty from beggin'. If you just let your hair get knotted once in a while . . . stop brushing it for gawd's sake! And try hobblin' a bit. There's plenty to be earned for a beggar with a limp. And a cough. Why don't you try coughin' a little —"

"I ain't beggin' or stealin' no more," Lizzie interrupted him sharply. "It ain't no life."

She wasn't going to pretend to have a cough for anyone. Ma had died from a cough last year. Grief pinched at Lizzie's heart as she remembered her mother spitting up blood, half-delirious with fever. Lizzie had pleaded with Pa to let her stay home and look after Ma. But Pa had dragged her onto the streets, making use of her tear-stained face to squeeze money from tenderhearted passersby.

Lizzie had known that Pa had money in his pocket that day, but he wouldn't spend it on a doctor for Ma — he was saving it to spend on gin. Ma had to cough and sweat alone, without even a sip of brandy to ease her suffering.

At least I was with her at the end. Lizzie closed her eyes, remembering how soft Ma's hair had felt. Tears pricked her eyes as the memories filled her mind, but she blinked them away — she wasn't going to let Pa see her cry. Like Ma said when her brother, John, had died three years ago, "You can waste the day cryin', or you can tuck him safe in your heart and let his memory keep you warm."

Lizzie shoved the memory away. She couldn't bring John back. Or Ma. But they were both safe in her heart.

Pa's boots scraped the floor. "What do you mean, you ain't beggin' or stealin' no more?"

Lizzie heard a ripping noise. She looked up with a gasp and saw her father clutching a handful of paper streamers.

"No!" she cried, leaping up and grabbing his arm. But it was too late. He'd already torn them and flung them onto the floor.

"My flower paper!" Lizzie dropped to her knees and began snatching it up frantically. "I was going to earn enough to get out of here."

"Get out of here?" With a heavy boot, Pa began to grind the paper into the grime. "Why do you want to get out of 'ere? Are you too good for the Castle, mi'lady?"

"I'm done with stealin' and beggin'!" Lizzie jumped to her feet. "I wish *you* were too!" Trembling with rage, she grabbed the jar off the table and splashed vinegar over Pa's soap-covered legs. The soap bubbled and frothed till his legs looked leprous with ulcers.

"That's what you wanted, ain't it?" Lizzie shrieked. She'd seen him use the soap-and-vinegar trick a hundred times. Fake sores earned more pennies to spend on gin. "With legs like that, you'll earn enough to drink yourself silly!"

Pa growled, and Lizzie swallowed, scared. What had she done? Pa's shins were dripping with froth, and fear dropped like a stone into the pit of her belly as his face hardened into a scowl. She knew what he could do; she'd watched him beat Ma and John enough times.

He lunged at her. "You ungrateful guttersnipe!"

Lizzie ducked.

"Get back here!" he roared.

Before she could duck again, his hand hit her cheek. It sent her reeling backward, and she knocked against the wall, making plates rattle on the shelves.

Half-blind with pain, she saw Pa coming at her again, his face dark with fury. Terror flared through her, and she dove between his legs and darted for the door. Fingers tugged at her skirt, but Lizzie tore free and raced out into the hall. She ran down the stairs, taking them three at a time. Her father's boots thundered after her, but she didn't look back as she burst out into the street.

People jostled along the narrow lane, and Lizzie slipped between them, bobbing and weaving, nimble as a prizefighter, until Pa's roars had faded far behind her. Heart thumping, she stumbled to a halt and leaned against a wall. People passed, but no one looked twice at her. Rat's Castle was filled with street urchins — for all anyone knew, Lizzie was just another pickpocket fleeing from the police.

She loosened her shawl, hot from running. Thank heaven it'd been a freezing night. The hard April frost meant she'd gone to her bed wearing every piece of clothing she owned. If it had been summer, she'd be in her nightgown.

Lizzie looked about, wondering which way to go. A man was herding a pig along the muddy lane. Two washerwomen heaved sacks of clothing on their backs, bent under their weight. A rosy-cheeked fellow balanced a tray in the crook of his arm. "Hot sheeps' feet!" he called.

The delicious smell made Lizzie's mouth water, but her pockets were empty. She glanced down the lane, terrified that she would see her father's face.

"Lizzie?" A wrinkled hand grasped her sleeve. "Spare some change?"

Lizzie pulled away, recognizing one of the old crones who begged outside their building. "I've got nothing."

"Is that Lizzie Brown?" A blind old man was tapping his way toward her with a cane.

She had to hide — this pair would sell her back to Pa for a penny. She hopped over the gutter and ducked between the washerwomen's bulging sacks. Keeping low, she shadowed them this way and that as they wound their way through the alleys of Rat's Castle. She passed closed doors, boarded windows, and narrow passageways. Above her, the sky was no more than a strip of blue between the crowded roofs.

Where could she hide? She didn't have a penny on her, and she would need one for an inn or a room. Thanks to her father, she knew how to snatch watches or handkerchiefs, but she was determined no one would make a pickpocket of her. Mud splashed her boots as she followed the chattering washerwomen.

One of them glanced back at her, frowning suspiciously. "What you followin' us for?" she snapped.

"I wasn't followin' you!" Lizzie protested.

"Get away!" the woman hollered.

As the washerwoman lifted a hand to clip her ear, Lizzie darted down an alley. Hardly wide enough to squeeze through, it ran between ramshackle houses. Light glowed at the end. Her heart lifting, Lizzie hurried along and burst out into the sunshine.

She blinked in the sudden brightness. Horse-drawn carriages whisked by, their wheels rattling. Men in stiff collars, wearing glittering watch chains, strode down wide, clean pavements. Women in stripes and ruffles twirled parasols as they passed gleaming shop windows.

Oxford Street.

After the filth and gloom of Rat's Castle, it was like stepping into another world.

CHAPTER 2

She'd escaped! Lizzie's heart soared as she stared at the bright, busy street, but then a sharp knock on the ankles sent her staggering.

"Move out of the way." The well-dressed gentleman hardly even looked at her as he pushed her aside with his silver-topped cane and marched past.

Lizzie heard a rattling noise beside her. She looked and saw pennies in a cup. A beggar, ragged and stinking, stood steps away, chin lifted proudly. A sign hanging limply around his neck read "Crippled in Crimea."

As he lifted his tin cup apologetically, a woman in a feathered hat slowed and opened her purse. She dropped a coin into the beggar's cup, then held another out to Lizzie.

"No! No, ma'am!" Lizzie backed away in horror. "I ain't askin' for your money." She turned and ran. As faces blurred around her, she pictured Pa grinning.

See, I told you so! he chuckled. *You're a beggar like me, and you'll never be anything more.*

"That's not true!" Lizzie sobbed. She didn't care if anyone heard her.

"Ee-ee-eels, alive-o!"

She tore past a man with a barrel strapped to his back. Eels slapped and sloshed inside. Lizzie clenched her fists. "I'll find work," she muttered. "I know I will!"

But how?

Blinded by tears, Lizzie raced along the gutter until the world suddenly opened around her. The buildings gave way to wide lawns, and she stumbled to a halt. Trees lined the far horizon. Birds swooped between their shimmering branches, and sunshine glittered on water in the distance.

The surprise of green grass and blue sky calmed Lizzie's panic. She had never even *imagined* anywhere this beautiful. *I found this all by myself!* Lizzie caught her breath. *And I'll find a new life too.*

Tilting her chin stubbornly, Lizzie marched toward the wrought-iron gates, where the road swept in among the lawns. People streamed around her, chattering excitedly. A woman in a feathered hat pushed ahead of her, pulling a well-dressed girl by the hand.

"What is this place?" Lizzie called to the girl.

"Hyde Park." The girl held onto her hat as a gang of boys jostled past.

"Where's everyone going?" Lizzie asked. The crowd was swarming through the gates, eager as folks hurrying to a music hall.

"Don't you know?" the girl cried, but the woman in the feathered hat jerked her away.

"Read all about it!" A paperboy waved a newspaper above his head. "The Phantom strikes again!"

"The Phantom?" A young woman in a bright red dress snatched the paper from the boy's hand.

"A penny, if you please." The boy held out his hand to her.

"Here." The woman fumbled in her purse, one eye on her paper.

The boy took her coin, tugged another paper from a bundle tucked under his arm, and flapped it in the air. "Police dumbfounded as Phantom gives them the slip!"

The Phantom? Lizzie craned to see.

A man in a narrow-brimmed hat was holding the woman in red's arm. "What's he done this time, Gladys?"

"Another burglary." Gladys pressed closer to the man. "Oh, Ernest! That's the fourth burglary this month, and no one's even found a footprint."

"Sliest burglar in London's history!" The paperboy pushed himself forward and began offering papers left and right. "No one knows how he gets in."

"Or out," Ernest muttered.

"He must be a ghost," Gladys gasped. "It says here that he got through three locked doors and broke into an uncrackable safe this time."

Lizzie stood on tiptoes and peeked at Gladys's paper. The headline read:

Phantom Targets Lowndes Square in Daring Jewel Theft

Swiftly skimming the article below, Lizzie picked
out the words she could read, just as Ma had taught her.
Robbery while the family slept . . . No sign of a break-in . . .
Famous London psychic, Mrs. Palfry, claims she saw him in a
dream . . . described his features to an artist. Below the words
was a sketch of the cruelest face Lizzie had ever seen. A
chill ran through her.

Ernest whistled. "That's no human face."

"Perhaps it's a mask," Gladys suggested.

"I hope so." Ernest tucked his arm protectively around
her narrow waist.

Music suddenly sounded from outside the park
gates. As Lizzie turned around, the crowd parted and she
glimpsed a man in a red spangled jacket. Behind him, a riot
of noise and color filled the road.

A parade!

Lizzie hurried to the side of the road and pressed
in with the crowd, her eyes wide as a huge gray animal
lumbered past. She'd only ever seen them in pictures
before — an elephant, a real one! It was huge, with a big
round belly and a long, dangling trunk. It was draped in
colorful silk and crowned with a seat as ornate as any
carriage. A lady waved from the top.

"Roll up!" The man in the spangled jacket was waving
a long, golden baton. "Roll up for Fitzy's Traveling Circus.

Watch death-defying stunts! Marvel at acrobatic feats never seen before. See Sullivans' Bareback Balleta. Be amazed by Anita, the World's Smallest Woman. Mermaids, camels, elephants, and lions — Fitzy's Circus has got it all!"

More elephants lumbered past, followed by the band. A big bass drum bounced on the belly of a fat man. Cymbals flashed in the sunshine, and trumpets blasted in time to the beat. Then came six golden horses, their riders glittering in matching jackets.

Lizzie stared up at them, mouth open. One was a girl about her own age with flaming red hair that streamed down her back. What must it feel like to be up there on horseback? The girl suddenly caught Lizzie's eye. She grinned, then threw her feet skyward and balanced on her saddle in a graceful handstand. Lizzie clapped wildly.

"Look, Ma!" A young boy squeezed past Lizzie and pointed at the final carriage, which rumbled behind the riders.

Lizzie dragged her gaze from the girl on horseback. Through the iron bars of the carriage, she could see a light brown animal pacing. It was making a loud snarling noise, and its tail swished back and forth menacingly. A sign above the cage read "King of the Jungle."

"Alfred, you get back here!" The boy's mother grabbed his hand and tugged him away.

Lizzie stood, rooted to the spot, as the dazzling parade flowed past. Acrobats balanced on each other's shoulders.

Clowns tumbled and teased the crowd, squirting water from flowers and pulling pennies from behind children's ears. Lizzie clasped her hands against her heart. Surely she could find some work here? There were animals to be fed, cages to be cleaned out, and costumes to be laundered. Her mind whirled with possibilities as she watched the circus disappear into the park.

Kids were dodging through the crowd, handing out fliers as they yelled, "First show at dusk!" and "Bring the family! Threepenny a ticket. Five tickets for a shilling!"

Lizzie hardly heard them. She was too busy following the trail of muck and rutted earth the circus had left in its wake. By the time she caught up, the carriages were parked. The dazzling showmen were leaping down from their boxes and stripping off their fancy jackets. As Lizzie watched, a dozen burly men, sleeves rolled up, heaved a huge bundle of red-and-black striped canvas from the back of a cart. Shouting back and forth to one another, they began to unfold it, and before long, they were winching the round, pointed roof of a circus tent into the bright blue sky.

"Hey, Joss! Pass a mallet!" A curly haired man heaved a rope to another man and hooked the end around a loose wooden peg. His muscles strained as he held it in place.

Quickly, Lizzie scanned the grass. A mallet was lying just a few feet away. She raced to it and dragged it across the grass. "Here!"

The curly haired man glanced quickly over his shoulder. "Knock this peg in before this rope pulls it back out, love."

Lizzie heaved the mallet as high as she could and let it drop onto the peg. The peg sank deep into the soft earth.

"Thanks." The man let go of the rope and rubbed the sweat from his brow. Then he frowned at Lizzie. "Who are you?"

"I'm Lizzie Brown." She looked at him hopefully. "Is there anything else I can do?"

"You can stay out the way." The man waved her away. "The tent's not safe till every peg's driven in."

"I'll be careful," Lizzie promised.

"Girls ain't no good for heavy work." The man strode away, not looking back.

Lizzie stuck out her tongue. "I hammered that peg in for you, didn't I?" She glanced around and spotted a woman struggling to drape a striped canvas over a wooden booth. "Let me help." She grabbed a corner of the woman's tent and began pulling it.

"Get off!" the woman snapped. "You'll tear it!"

Lizzie let go. "I was only tryin' to help."

"Go help somewhere else." The woman turned her back.

Lizzie's heart sank. Wasn't there anything she could do? Around her, the site rang with the sounds of hammering and cursing. Sideshows began to dot the field

around the big tent, and beyond them, Lizzie could see
the great frames of the swing-boats and roundabouts
silhouetted against the horizon. Perhaps once everything
was set up, she'd be able to find some way to earn her
supper. She wandered to the edge of the field and sank
into the grass.

The sun was warm now, and the low hedge behind
shielded her from the breeze. Lizzie watched the circus
grow, studying faces and voices, trying to guess where the
most work was and who'd be most likely to give it to her.
A woman sat sewing up a tear in a wide sheet of canvas.
Another was building a fire in front of her stall. There had
to be some way to win their trust, but right now Lizzie
couldn't think of one.

The sun slid across the sky until she felt her eyelids
droop. Exhausted, Lizzie let her thoughts drift and, within
minutes, she was dozing, and dreaming.

*The alleys and doorways of Rat's Castle twisted and snaked
at the edge of her dreams. Her breath quickened as she saw eyes
flashing from the shadows. She pelted forward into darkness
and ran blind. Suddenly the Phantom loomed ahead of her. His
grotesque face grinned a breath away from hers, a smile twisting
his lips. . . .*

Lizzie opened her eyes with a start. The nightmare had
been so vivid she had to keep blinking to make sure the
face wasn't really there. She shook her head to chase away
the terrifying image. Nightmares were nothing new to

Lizzie. She'd always had vivid dreams, and when she was little she'd loved to tell her mother about them when she woke up. But since Ma had died, her dreams had become darker and even more realistic.

It was dark now, and crowds were swarming toward the circus. Music thrummed from the big striped tent. Stallholders hollered beside their booths. The swing-boat swooped up and down against the night sky, squeals of terror exploding with each drop of the gondola.

"You'll catch cold on that damp grass."

Lizzie looked up at the sound of a voice. An old man with a kind smile was standing over her.

"I'm fine," she said, scrambling to her feet.

"Here." He held out a tin mug filled to the brim with hot soup. "This'll keep the chill off."

Lizzie stared at the soup warily. The man was dressed like a gentleman, but his voice had the twang of Rat's Castle. Lizzie said, "What do you want for it? I ain't got no money."

The man pressed the mug gently into her hands. "Just give the cup back to the soup-seller when you're done." He nodded toward a small canvas booth set up nearby. A woman, sleeves rolled, stirred a large iron pot hanging over a fire.

Lizzie narrowed her eyes. What if he was one of those do-gooders? He might make her go home to Pa. Or to an orphanage. Or to the workhouse. But the soup smelled good, and her belly was rumbling. She leaned over it and let the steam warm her face.

"Here." He slid a penny into her palm. "Treat yourself."

Lizzie backed away. "I ain't a beggar, sir."

"I know." The man gazed at her steadily. "But I was poor and hungry when I was your age, so I know how it feels."

Lizzie watched him walk away. The hot mug stung her hands and the soup burned her lips, but she swallowed anyway. She was so hungry it was worth the scalding.

By the time she finished, Lizzie felt warmer. The lights from the circus flickered enticingly. Shaking the dampness from her skirt, she crossed the grass. "Thanks, missus." She offered the mug to the soup-seller.

The woman took it without looking up. "Better hurry, dearie. Next show is the last show."

Lizzie hadn't realized it was so late. Had she really slept so long? She hurried among the booths, peeking past the canvas doorways held open by their owners.

"Walk in! Walk in!" A stallholder brandished an ivory cane. "Come and see the Pig-Faced Woman!" Lizzie strained to see into the shadowy tent. Above the door, a painted sign showed a picture of a woman dressed in a crinoline. Lace cuffs framed pretty hands, but above the collar the woman had a snout, beady eyes, and pointy ears that poked out from under her hair.

"Come on, dearie," the stallholder enticed. "Just a penny to see one of the Wonders of the World."

Lizzie clutched her penny in her palm.

"See the world's only captive mermaid!" another stallholder hollered. "Come inside and watch her comb her golden hair while she flaps her fishy tail."

Lizzie glanced from the Mermaid to the Pig-Faced Woman. She only had one penny. Which one should she choose?

Then another sign caught her eye:

Ten in One

"I spy a curious young lady." A showman twirled the waxed tips of his moustache between his fingers. "Come closer, my dear. See ten amazing acts for just one penny!"

Ten amazing acts.

Without hesitating, Lizzie headed straight for his tent, handed over her penny, and ducked inside.

Visitors clustered in front of the small stages, their faces glowing in the gaslight. Eagerly, Lizzie wriggled her way into the nearest crowd. As she popped out at the front, she saw a man standing bare-chested beside a smoldering fire. With a flourish, he lit a long taper on the burning coals and lowered the flame into his mouth.

Lizzie gasped as he closed his lips around it. He stared at her with sparkling eyes, then opened his mouth to let out a cloud of steam. Where was the flame? Lizzie watched in awe as he relit his taper, opened his mouth, and extinguished it again as easily as snuffing a candle.

What other wonders were waiting for her to see? Lizzie pushed her way to the next stage where a miniature rocking chair creaked in front of a small fireplace. A tiny hearth rug covered the stage, and little curtains dressed tiny windows painted on the backdrop. It looked like a parlor built for a child, and the woman seated in the rocking chair was not much bigger than a doll. She rocked back and forth in her chair, sucking on a clay pipe and reading a newspaper on her knee. Above the stage, the sign read:

Anita, the World's Smallest Woman

Lizzie struggled to get a better look, but the crowds were too thick for her to see through. Then, to her amazement, Anita noticed her and waved. "Let the little one through to the front please, ladies and gents!" she called. "She's paid her penny, same as you."

People laughed and shuffled aside to let her forward.

Lizzie beamed up at Anita. "You're real!" she said.

"Well, I ain't made of wood, if that's what you were wonderin' about." Anita winked.

A gasp burst from the crowd beside her. Lizzie turned to the next stage and saw an old man dressed in nothing but a loincloth. With a serene smile, he hopped from one foot to the other on a pile of glass shards.

His feet must be shredded, Lizzie thought. But the glass shards sparkled clear as fresh water with no sign of blood.

A showman strutted in front of the stage. "I discovered this ancient fakir in the mountains of Persia. Each morning he bathes in Epsom salts, and each night he drinks a potion of Eastern herbs which makes his skin as tough as leather."

Lizzie stared at the old man's skin. It did indeed seem as brown and weather-beaten as a leather glove. She turned, breathless with amazement, and saw a tall woman, black as ebony and tall as a giant. The sign above her read:

The Amazon Queen

Just then a blade flashed at the corner of Lizzie's eye. On the next stage, a man was tilting his head back and sliding a sword down his throat until the hilt rested on his lips.

Lizzie's eyes widened. In the circus, anything could happen. Surely there could be some small place here for her?

CHAPTER 3

Silk rustled behind her and Lizzie whirled around. A smiling woman — hefty as a draft horse and done up in brightly colored ruffles — was shooing her toward the exit. The other visitors were already streaming out of the tent.

"But I just got in!' Lizzie protested. "I haven't seen it all!"

"Then come back tomorrow," the woman said. "Why don't you pop along to the big tent? The last performance'll be starting any moment. We're closing up here. Poor Anita is exhausted."

"You're right about that, Flora. I'm worn to the bone." In her miniature parlor, Anita slid forward in her tiny chair and began rubbing her feet with small, plump hands. "I've lost all feeling in my toes." She hopped to the ground and began to limp toward her pint-sized fireplace.

In the tall booth opposite, the Amazon Queen pulled off her feather-and-bone headdress and dusted down her skirt. She called to Anita. "Come for your dinner at my wagon, 'Nita. I'll be makin' stew."

Lizzie stared in surprise. The Amazon Queen — twice as tall as Lizzie and as exotic as a bird of paradise — spoke with a raucous East End accent. "I thought she was from Africa!" Lizzie said.

"She is." Flora folded her hands and leaned back proudly. "I taught her English myself. Quick learner, she was."

The Amazon Queen gave a throaty laugh. "In Africa I speak like a queen. In England I speak like a washerwoman."

"What do you mean?" Flora threw up her arms. "Queen Victoria herself don't speak no better than me."

The Amazon Queen ignored her and nodded regally to the old man, then the sword swallower. "Why don't you both join us too? And if you'd be so kind as to bring a lil' somethin' to throw in the pot, we'll have a proper meal."

Lizzie felt a nudge from behind. It was Flora again. "You still here? Go find your ma. She'll be missin' you."

Flora shooed her out with the rest of the visitors, and before she could argue, Lizzie found herself outside. Purple clouds streaked a pink sky. An evening chill was flooding Hyde Park, and Lizzie shivered in the cold. She lifted her wool skirt, pulling it tight around her shoulders like a shawl and leaving her tattered petticoats to flutter around her legs.

The crowds were thinning as the last of the sideshow visitors filtered into the big tent. A top-hatted man in a patchwork waistcoat beckoned latecomers through the brightly lit entrance. "Last show! Last show!" He swapped their coins for tickets and waved them inside where flickering lights swallowed them.

Lizzie's shoulders drooped. Her purse was as empty as her belly. Heart heavy, she wandered across the grass while figures worked around her, closing up the sideshows and lighting lamps outside the caravans. Canvas flapped in the breeze, while music swelled inside the big tent, and a happy roar rose from the crowd. The show was about to begin.

Lizzie stopped beside a flower bed thick with bushes and stared across the field. This would be a safe place to rest. She sank to the ground and crawled beneath one of the bushes. The bruise on her cheek ached as the cold jabbed at it. But she knew Pa would give her another if she went home.

Curling up tight as a hedgehog, Lizzie listened to the ringmaster calling out the first act as stones grated against her bony arms. The crowd cheered while Lizzie snuggled deeper into her petticoats, trying to escape the cold and imagining what was happening inside the circus tent.

Lizzie carried on sitting there long after the show had finished and the audience had gone home. An owl screeched overhead and made her gasp. Aching all over, she crept out from beneath the bush into a sleeping world. The big tent flapped eerily in the darkness, and here and there caravan windows showed lights, but no one stirred. The owl screeched again, and Lizzie's teeth began to chatter. She had to find somewhere warmer.

Quiet as a mouse, she crept between the tents and caravans. A horse stamped beside her, making her jump. Warmth pulsed from its flanks. Heavy-hooved and clumsy with sleep, it knocked against her. Lizzie backed away past a caravan and glanced up at its door. Light shone from a small pane of glass, and laughter sounded inside. Lizzie could smell the mouthwatering scent of food. She wondered if the Amazon Queen was inside, eating dinner with the World's Smallest Woman.

The horse whinnied and thrust its head toward her inquisitively. Lizzie darted back, slipping into the shadows beside the big tent. She followed the striped canvas away from the booths and caravans. In the quiet moonlight, she saw animals shifting about in makeshift wooden pens. They huffed and sighed, breathing softly with sleep.

Lizzie leaned over a fence. A small herd of ponies was bunched together, their coats golden in the moonlight as they dozed. In the pen beside them, two huge beasts paced the grass. Lizzie stared at their long gangly legs. Then she saw the huge humps on their backs.

"Blimey!" Lizzie whispered. "God must've been havin' a laugh when he made you." The creatures paused and gazed at her with huge, dark eyes. Then they carried on pacing, their broad, soft feet silent on the grass.

A breeze lifted Lizzie's hair and made her shiver.
Spotting a gap between the pens, she squeezed into it,
eager to be out of the biting wind. She felt hay beneath her
feet and sank gratefully into it. In the pen beside her, the
two strange creatures tucked their legs clumsily beneath
them and settled down for the night. Lizzie could feel their
warmth through the slats of the fence. Wriggling closer,
she closed her eyes and rested, relaxing to the sound of
their soft breathing.

* * *

"Hey!"

Lizzie sat up with a jolt as a stick jabbed her ribs. Her
first thought was, *Pa's going to hit me again.*

Two feet stood beside her. One foot was small; the
other was large and misshapen. She looked up with a gasp
and saw a face frowning down.

The stick jabbed her again. It wasn't Pa, but Lizzie's
heart was still pounding. She pushed the stick away. "Get
off!" She leaped to her feet. "Stop it!" She found herself
staring into the eyes of a skinny boy, smaller than she was.
"There's no need to keep poking me," she muttered.

The boy glared down at her. "You shouldn't be here,"
he said.

"I was just leaving anyway." Dawn was lighting the sky
behind the big tent. Lizzie stepped forward. "Let me past."

"What's going on here?" A man sauntered up behind the scowling boy and looked Lizzie up and down. She recognized the man from the big tent. He was still wearing his patchwork waistcoat and top hat. "What have you found here, Mally?"

"She was sleeping in the hay," the boy answered without taking his eyes off Lizzie.

"We don't want that, do we, Malachy, m'boy?" The man's eyes twinkled. "If we feed the animals girl-flavored hay they might develop a taste for young 'uns."

Lizzie glanced anxiously at the strange animals in the pen. "They wouldn't eat me, would they?" she asked.

Malachy laughed. "They eat hay, not girls."

The man rested his hand on Malachy's shoulder. "I reckon a lion might enjoy her." He tipped his head to one side. "Though there's not much meat on her."

Lizzie backed away. "I-I'm sorry I slept here, but I . . ."

"Now, now, little 'un." The man nudged his hat so it sat back on his head. "We don't mean any harm."

Malachy shifted his misshapen foot. "Sorry I poked you so hard." He lifted his walking stick apologetically. Now he'd stopped glaring, his thin face looked more mischievous than unkind. "I thought you were a stray dog." He reached over the fence and patted one of the strange animals. "Dogs worry the animals."

Lizzie looked down at her shabby gray dress with dismay. "You thought I was a stray dog?"

Malachy flushed. "Sorry."

The man smiled at her. "I'm Edward Fitzgerald. Most people call me Fitzy. And this is my son, Malachy."

Lizzie stuck out her hand. "I'm Lizzie."

"Pleased to meet you, Lizzie." Mr. Fitzgerald reached past Malachy and shook Lizzie's hand. "What are you doing here? Are you lost?"

"No." Lizzie lifted her chin. "I'm looking for work."

Mr. Fitzgerald rubbed his chin. "You look a bit skinny to be any good for hard work."

"I've worked since I was seven years old," Lizzie retorted.

Malachy looked at his father. "Why don't we give her a try?" he suggested. "You were saying just this morning there's more work than hands around here."

"Workers cost money," Mr. Fitzgerald said with a frown.

"I don't need much," Lizzie told him quickly. "And I'll tell you what — I'll work for a whole week for you without takin' a penny, just for food. If you don't think I'm worth it by then, I'll go away quiet."

Mr. Fitzgerald looked her up and down again. "I don't know about that."

"I'm a hard worker," Lizzie urged.

"Go on, Pop," Malachy chimed in.

Mr. Fitzgerald scratched his head. "All right, then. I'll give you a trial."

"You won't be sorry!" Lizzie wanted to hug him.

"You can't sleep here, though," Fitzy went on.

Lizzie glanced at the sky. "It's nearly dawn," she pointed out. "I don't need more sleep. I can start work now if you like." She wanted to prove she was strong and willing.

"Breakfast first," Mr. Fitzgerald said. "Take her to Ma Sullivan, Mally," he called over his shoulder as he ducked down and disappeared under the canvas wall of the big tent.

"Follow me." Malachy began to walk toward the caravans. His curly hair was cropped close to his head, and his body was wiry beneath his shirt and breeches. Despite the heavy boot on his misshapen foot, he moved fast, and Lizzie had to run to keep up, swerving around ropes and jumping over tent pegs as she went.

The circus was already awake. A caravan door opened as they passed and a clown peered out.

"I thought everyone'd sleep late," Lizzie called after Malachy. "They must have worked till near midnight."

"Dawn's the best chance the performers get to practice," Malachy answered. "No passersby gawking."

Two burly men with rolled-up sleeves crossed Lizzie's path, and she stopped to let them by. One of them carried a heavy coil of rope slung across his chest. The other was wheeling a penny-farthing bicycle with a huge front wheel. An elegant young woman wrapped in a brightly embroidered shawl glided behind them, and Lizzie gasped as she passed.

Malachy stopped and spun around. "What's the matter?"

Lizzie pointed at the young woman. "She's got no clothes on!" Beneath the shawl she could see the young woman's legs clad in nothing but spangled tights. "Where are her petticoats?"

"That's her costume." Malachy laughed. "She can't practice in petticoats."

"Practice what?"

"She rides that bicylce on the high wire."

Lizzie gasped. "Not really!"

Malachy grinned. "Her act is near the beginning of the show." He pointed to a group of wiry youths turning somersaults, and Lizzie recognized the acrobats from the parade. "They usually come after her," he told her.

Nearby, Lizzie noticed a boy cantering in a circle on one of the golden ponies. As she watched, the boy leaped up and balanced on his hands on the back of the prancing pony, just like the red-haired girl from the parade. "Lordy!" She stared in wonder. "Does everyone here have an act?"

Malachy tapped his clumpy foot with his stick. "Everyone except me."

Lizzie glanced down, wondering what to say.

"Don't worry." Malachy shrugged. "I got extra brains instead."

Before Lizzie could speak, Malachy grabbed her arm and tugged her sideways. "Keep your eyes peeled around here." He pointed to one of the elephants swaying heavily toward them. "If you get trampled it's your own fault."

"It's huge!" Lizzie's heart lurched as it tramped so close that she felt the air stir around her. Its ears flapped like wings, and its wrinkly flesh rippled with each thumping step. She gripped onto Malachy as the ground shook beneath her feet. "Does it trample many people?"

Malachy laughed. "Only people daft enough not to see her coming."

A tiny Indian man followed behind the elephant. He wore a vest and carried a broom in one hand and a cake of soap in the other. "Good morning, Malachy," he called.

"Morning, Zezete." Malachy patted the elephant. "Morning, Akula." The animal lifted its trunk and trumpeted loudly.

Lizzie covered her ears. Then her nose. The stench following the animal made her eyes water.

"Akula's going for her bath." Malachy shielded his eyes. "I hope the park keepers aren't awake yet. I don't know if they'd approve of her bathing in their pond."

Lizzie giggled. "Can we watch?"

"Don't be rude!" Malachy grinned. "Poor Akula's shy about bath time. She worries about her weight."

As his eyes flashed teasingly, Lizzie felt a jab of grief — that was the sort of silly thing her brother John would have said. She pushed the thought away and asked, "Ain't they dangerous, with those big twisty teeth?"

"No," said Malachy. "They may be big, but they're gentle as anything. Not like the lion." He pointed toward the wagon with iron bars that Lizzie had seen on the parade. "That's Leo's cage," he told her. "He's our lion."

"Why's it empty?" Lizzie glanced nervously over her shoulder.

Malachy leaned close. "He escaped last night," he whispered. "We've been looking for him ever since." Without waiting for a response, he crossed the grass and stopped outside a bright yellow caravan. "Nora! Erin!" he called up the ladder steps.

A curly redheaded girl poked out of the door. "What?"

"Come and meet Lizzie," Malachy said.

The head ducked back inside. "Nora!"

"The Sullivans are the best bareback riders in Europe," Malachy told Lizzie as she caught up. "That was Conor you saw practicing on the pony."

Lizzie heard the door open again, and two identical girls, both rosy-cheeked and with thick red hair, stepped out of the caravan.

"Hello," said the first girl with a kind smile. "I'm Nora."

"And I'm Erin." Her twin sister pushed ahead and grabbed Lizzie's hand, shaking it enthusiastically. "Pleased to meet you."

"Excuse me!" Nora elbowed Erin aside. "Forgive my sister." Her blue eyes twinkled as she spoke. "She's got no manners."

"I do too!" Erin objected.

"Do not." Nora put her hands on her hips and faced Erin squarely. "No manners at all."

Malachy slid between them. "Before you start fighting, I was hoping your ma could find a bit of breakfast for Lizzie."

"Is she staying?" Nora asked.

"Is she joining the circus?" Erin chimed in. Their squabble forgotten, they both turned toward Lizzie, faces eager for answers. "What's your act?"

"High wire," Nora guessed.

"No, no," Erin butted in. "She's not got enough flesh on her." She squeezed the muscles on Lizzie's arm.

Lizzie pulled away. "I — I don't have an act."

"Not yet," Nora said. "But Fitzy will find you a speciality before long."

Erin laughed. "Even if it's just balancing on Akula's trunk!"

Nora nodded. "She could do that. She looks light as a feather."

"What is going on out here?" a voice interrupted them suddenly.

Lizzie looked up the caravan steps as a ruddy-cheeked woman appeared in the doorway with her hands on her hips. Strands of dark hair whisked around her flashing blue eyes.

Nora raced toward the woman and reached up the caravan steps to tug on the hem of her skirts. "Can Lizzie have breakfast with us, Ma? Fitzy just hired her."

Lizzie looked shyly up at Nora's mother. "If you've not got nothin' to spare, I'll be fine," she lied. Her belly was growling.

"There's always a bit to spare in the Sullivan family," Ma Sullivan said, looking over her shoulder. "Move over, Patrick. Sean, make some space. There's going to be an extra kiddie at the table."

Before she knew what was happening, Lizzie felt Erin and Nora bundling her up the caravan stairs. Inside, the walls were lined with cupboards and shelves. A stove was squeezed in the corner beside the door, and in the middle was a table. Two dark-haired boys with lean, muscular arms were wrestling across the top of it, while a man sucked on a pipe, half-hidden by a newspaper at the far end.

"Patrick, Sean, you best behave yourselves," Ma ordered.

Grumbling, the two boys slid back into their seats.

"Those are two of my brothers," Erin said. "And that's Pa."

Pa lifted his pipe. "Welcome to the Sullivan Palace," he called and went back to his paper.

"Ma opens up the tea tent after ten in the morning," said Nora. "If you work at Fitzy's, you can go there for a meal or a brew any time."

One of the boys reached out and ruffled Erin's hair fondly. "Don't tell me you've brought home another stray puppy." He winked at Lizzie.

"Patrick Sullivan, don't be rude to our guest!" Erin said.

"Lizzie's come for breakfast," Nora added, flashing a challenging stare at Sean. "So no playing any of your pranks on her."

Sean held up his hands. "It's Brendan and Conor you need to be warning, not us."

Nora shook her hair from her face. "And so I will when they get back from practice."

Ma Sullivan pushed her way to the stove and pulled a pot from the heat. "I hope you like porridge, Lizzie."

Lizzie's stomach growled in reply.

"I'd say that sounds like a yes," Pa said from behind his paper.

* * *

After breakfast, Lizzie plopped down in the grass and leaned against the tall, spoked wheel of the caravan. She felt sleepy with her belly full and the sun shining warm on her face.

Nora settled beside her. "Ma wants you to stay with us. She won't have any child sleep outside when we can make room."

"Are you sure?" Lizzie wondered how the six Sullivan children and Ma and Pa managed to sleep in that small caravan as it was.

"Look." Nora wriggled between the wheels and opened a door to a wide square compartment underneath the caravan.

Lizzie's eyes widened. "We don't have to sleep in there, do we?"

Nora spluttered with laughter. "No, silly! We pack all the costumes and knickknacks here in the bellybox. Then there's room to make up the bunk beds. You can squeeze between Erin and me. We'll be as snug as bedbugs."

The caravan creaked as Pa settled himself on the steps and carried on reading his newspaper.

Lizzie lay back in the grass and closed her eyes. She'd be warm tonight and surrounded by new friends. Smiling, she listened to the sounds of the circus. Horses whinnied, Akula trumpeted, and somewhere there was a snarling noise.

Lizzie sat up with a jerk. "Lion!"

"What's the matter, Lizzie?" Erin asked, leaping down past Pa.

Nora leaned close. "You look like you've seen a ghost!" she said.

"The lion!" Lizzie jumped to her feet and stared around, heart racing. Was that a flash of golden mane behind the feed wagon? "The escaped lion!"

"What escaped lion?" Nora was staring at her as though she were mad.

"Leo! His cage was empty! Malachy said he'd escaped!"

"Escaped?" Pa slapped his thigh, laughing. "Oh, Leo's too old to escape, and even if he did he's got no teeth, nor sense enough to harm a lamb. Malachy's been pulling your leg —"

Pa Sullivan broke off suddenly, his attention fixed on his paper. "Lord preserve us!" He jabbed the paper with his finger. "He's held a candle to the devil this time."

"Who has?" Erin raced to his side.

"The Phantom," Pa said.

The Phantom? Lizzie forgot the lion at once.

"Did you say the Phantom?" Patrick appeared at the caravan door, eyes bright. "Has he cracked another safe?" he asked, grinning.

"Patrick Sullivan!" Erin said, frowning at her brother. "Safe-cracking is not a sport, y'know! The Phantom's a wicked burglar, and he's going straight to jail when they catch him."

"Let's hope they catch him soon," Pa Sullivan said grimly.

"Why?" Erin peered at her father's paper. "What's he done this time?"

"He's turned nasty, that's what," Pa growled. "Some poor fella in Spitalfields went blundering in on him while he was robbing a house. Got bashed over the head for his trouble and left for dead."

Erin grasped Pa's arm. "Did the Phantom kill him?"

"Close enough," Pa muttered.

Nora squeezed closer to Lizzie. "Why do folks say he's a ghost, Pa?" Her blue eyes were wide with fear.

"'Cos they're daft," Lizzie said, hooking her arm around Nora. "There's no such thing as ghosts. He's flesh and blood like anyone else." She'd never believed in superstitious nonsense, and she wasn't about to start now.

CHAPTER 4

"You've settled in, then?"

Mr. Fitzgerald's voice made Lizzie jump. She scrambled to her feet. "They've been heavenly kind, Mr. Fitzgerald."

"Call me Fitzy. Everyone else does." Mr. Fitzgerald lifted his top hat to Mr. Sullivan. "Thanks for feeding an extra mouth, Rory."

Mr. Sullivan shook out his paper. "One more makes no difference."

"She's gonna stay with us," Nora chimed in. "There's room in our bunk."

"Glad to hear it." Mr. Fitzgerald reached into his jacket pocket and drew out a roll of papers. "Now, Lizzie, I want you to go and paste up some bills around town."

Nora clapped her hands. "Can we help?"

"I've got flour paste in the bellybox!" Erin dove beneath the wagon and wriggled out a moment later holding a jam jar and a paintbrush. "Leftovers from sticking last week's clippings in the scrapbook."

"If there's three of you, sell some tickets while you're out." Mr. Fitzgerald pulled a roll of tickets from his pocket and gave them to Lizzie. "Threepence a ticket . . ."

". . . five for a shilling," Lizzie chanted.

Mr. Fitzgerald winked. "Exactly."

Pa Sullivan wagged a finger at Erin and Nora. "Make sure you're back in time for practice."

"Yes, Pa!" Erin was already dashing away over the grass with Nora at her heels.

Lizzie raced after them, puffing by the time she reached the park gates. Erin and Nora were already pasting a bill onto a pillar. It read:

Fitzy's Traveling Circus
Every Evening at Dusk
The Astonishing Boissets
Mario the Mighty
Sullivans' Bareback Balleta

"That's us," Nora pointed to the Balleta. "We perform a whole ballet on horseback, costume changes an' all."

"Who's he?" Lizzie asked, pointing to a handsome young man. The bill said he was one of the Astonishing Boissets. With dark hair and shining eyes, he looked like a prince.

Erin and Nora looked at one another and giggled.

"Tell me!" Lizzie said, growing a little hot in the face.

"Tell you? We'll introduce you," Nora said with a grin.

"Keep a look out, Lizzie." Erin slapped another brushful of paste over the poster, covering the handsome youth with a blob of gloop. "Police don't like us bill-sticking."

"Leave it to me." Lizzie was used to playing lookout. She'd kept watch for Pa often enough while he'd been pulling one of his begging scams. She backed out into the road until she had a clear view of both sides of the park and could glance over her shoulder and see straight down Oxford Street. There was no sign of a blue uniform among the shoppers on Oxford Street, and the sidewalks beside the park were empty except for the occasional stroller or a nanny out for a bit of early morning air. "If I see a police officer I'll do this." Lizzie whistled a shrill warning.

Nora grinned. "I think we'll hear that a mile off."

Lizzie spotted a smartly dressed gent on Oxford Street. "Circus ticket, sir?" She crossed the road and fell into step beside him. "I'm sure your family would love to watch the World-Famous Bareback Balleta." The gent slowed, and Lizzie quickly tore off five tickets. "There's acrobats and elephants and humpbacked horses."

"Humpbacked horses?" The gent stopped.

"Like horses, but bigger and *much* humpier," Lizzie told him. "I seen them m'self. Big long noses and goo-goo eyes." She made a face, trying to show him how the odd animals had looked at her last night.

45

The gent suddenly smiled. "I think my family would enjoy seeing humpy horses with goo-goo eyes."

"Five tickets for a shilling." Lizzie held up the tickets and took his shilling. "Thank you kindly, sir." Grinning, she checked the roads again for police and headed toward another shopper. "Circus tickets, five for a shilling!"

* * *

Back at the circus, Lizzie jingled her dress pockets as she followed Fitzy around the outside of the big tent. They were heavy with coins. "I sold 'em all."

"I'm impressed!" Fitzy stepped over a rope and tugged it to make sure it was taut. "You're a natural."

"What can I do now?" Lizzie asked.

"Dump your coins there." Fitzy spread a handkerchief on the grass. "Then go give Anita a hand." He waved toward the Ten-in-One tent.

Lizzie emptied her pockets and hurried away, dodging between the stalls until she reached the Ten-in-One tent. As she burst through the door, Anita spun around on her stage.

"Hello," Lizzie panted. "Fitzy sent me to help." She glanced around the empty stages. "Where is everyone?"

"The show don't open till dusk," Anita said. "Hang about, I've seen you before, haven't I? You was in the audience last night."

"I'm Lizzie." She climbed onto the stage beside Anita.

The tiny woman waved toward her backdrop. "That needs changing. It's filthy, but I can't reach the hooks."

Lizzie reached up and began unhooking the backdrop from its hanger, keeping her eyes on her work. Anita was so small that she only reached Lizzie's waist, and Lizzie paused and stole a look at her. "I hope you don't mind my asking, but how come you're so tiny?"

"Never grew much since I was born." Anita sat down in her chair and pointed up at the backdrop. "Keep on unpinnin'."

Lizzie turned back to her work. "Don't you hate sitting here being stared at by strangers?" She shuddered. "I know I'd hate it."

"I did to begin with," Anita admitted. "But I'm used to it now. There's folks here who look out for me. Life here ain't as tough as it was out there."

Lizzie glanced over her shoulder. "What did you do?" she asked. "Out there I mean?" She wondered if Anita had lived anywhere as awful as Rat's Castle.

"I did what I could," Anita told her. "Beggin', mainly. No one'd give me proper work. And beggin' was no picnic. People used to throw things at me, kick me. Once someone picked me up and threw me. Like I was no more than a dog."

"Why do people have to be mean?" Lizzie asked. She unhooked the last hook and laid the backdrop on the stage.

Anita pointed to a fresh backdrop folded beside her chair. "I guess they don't know no better."

Lizzie scooped it up and began hooking.

"I'm glad Fitzy found me," the tiny woman told her. "Saw me beggin' and asked me to join his circus. Of course, I'd rather be a lady livin' in a big house with servants and all that, but I'm safe in my penny gaff."

Lizzie paused. "What's a penny gaff?"

"You're standing in one," Anita told her. "It's a sideshow. Something a person would pay a penny to see." A loud bell clanged outside, and Anita hopped off her chair. "That's Fitzy. Sounds like he's got an announcement."

Lizzie quickly finished hooking up the backdrop, then jumped down after Anita and crossed the field to where Fitzy was standing outside the big show tent.

The Fat Lady stood puffing beside him while the Amazon Queen sat on a barrel sewing fresh feathers onto her headdress. Show folk streamed from every wagon and tent, and Lizzie recognized the acrobats and clowns from the parade. Dwarves toddled beside giants. A boy on stilts stopped and leaned against a rope.

"Lizzie!" Erin and Nora came running across the grass.

Lizzie rushed to meet them. "What's Fitzy want?"

"Dunno." Erin shrugged.

"The mayor's here," Malachy said, ducking under a rope and stopping beside them. "He's come to see Pop."

"The Mayor of London?" Lizzie gasped. "Here?"

Nora grinned. "Our pa said he'd come."

"He's made friends with Pop," Malachy explained.

"Where is he?" Lizzie scanned the crowd until she saw an older gentleman step from the shadows behind Fitzy. Erin let out a loud whistle, and Malachy hooted as the crowd erupted into cheers.

"Hooray for His Lordship!"

"Long live the mayor!"

Lizzie stared open-mouthed — it was the old gentleman who'd given her soup and the penny. *The Lord Mayor of London!*

The mayor waved the crowd into silence. "Thank you for your warm welcome. I've come to tell you that when you set up at Victoria Park next month, I will lead the official opening ceremony!"

As the show folk burst into more cheering, Fitzy stepped forward and shouted, "Three cheers for the mayor!"

"Hip hip hooray!" Lizzie shouted with the crowd.

"Hip hip hooray!"

"Hip hip hooray!"

"The mayor's support will mean bigger audiences," Fitzy went on. "And better write-ups in the press. Victoria Park will be our best show ever!"

Malachy whispered in Lizzie's ear, "The papers don't usually have anything good to say about us circus folk."

"Now, back to work." Fitzy looked at his pocketwatch. "The first show starts in four hours."

As the crowd melted away, Malachy glanced at Lizzie. "How are you enjoying circus life?"

"It's brilliant!" Lizzie winked at him. "Almost worth being poked awake with a stick." Malachy looked sheepish, and Lizzie nudged him playfully. "I'm joking," she said. "I never thanked you for convincing your pa to take me on."

Malachy shrugged. "You're welcome." Lizzie thought she saw him blush as he turned and hobbled away between the booths.

Erin tugged Lizzie's sleeves. "You're coming to watch us practice, aren't you?"

"Next time," Lizzie promised. Right now, she wanted to make herself as useful as she could. She began to pick her way around the show tent, hopping over the ropes until she spotted a large man heaving a tall pole onto its end. She rushed to help.

"Let me hold it," Lizzie said. She ducked under the man's elbow and clung onto the pole, holding it in place while the man fixed its ropes onto pegs.

"You're strong for a little 'un." The man's voice was deep. Lizzie glanced at him and suddenly realized he was the tallest man she'd ever seen. He held out a huge hand for her to shake. "I'm Mario."

Lizzie stared up at him. "Mario the Mighty! From the poster! You're the circus giant."

He must be ten feet tall! Lizzie thought. She wondered what he'd look like standing next to Anita.

Mario nodded toward another tent pole. "If I lift that into place can you do some more holding while I fix the ropes?"

Lizzie nodded and braced herself, ready to take the weight of the pole as Mario heaved it up onto its end.

"Did you hear about the mayor?" Mario asked as he looped a rope around a peg.

Lizzie nodded and hugged the pole. "It's great that he's opening the circus in Victoria Park."

"If that don't bring the crowds in, nothing will." Mario grinned. "The mayor's a good 'un. He knows what it's like to come from poverty."

Lizzie pricked her ears. "Really?" She remembered the twang in the mayor's voice.

"He was raised in Jacob's Island," Mario told her.

Jacob's Island. Lizzie could hardly believe it. That was more of a slum than Rat's Castle. Pa used to say, "Just be grateful you ain't stuck in Jacob's Island. They feed their babies to dogs there."

Lizzie shivered. "How did he get out?"

"He worked his way out," Mario told her. "From errand boy to mayor and not a false step in between."

"I seen him the first night I was here," Lizzie told Mario. "He gave me soup and a penny. Best soup I ever tasted. I was starving."

Mario looked at her quizzically. "Where are you from?"

"Rat's Castle," Lizzie replied.

Mario shook his head and lifted another tent pole. "You're better off here."

Lizzie rushed to help balance it. "Don't I know it!"

"Poverty can do evil things to a man's soul."

Lizzie thought of Pa and shuddered.

* * *

"Is Harry here?" Lizzie peeked through the tent doorway. A foul stink hit her nose, and she covered it with her hand. It was the end of a long day. Dusk was falling, and the crowds were gathering outside.

A boy was sitting on a stool near an elephant. "I'm Hari," he said.

"Hari." Lizzie repeated the name, copying the boy's soft accent. It felt clumsy on her tongue.

"It's Indian," Hari explained.

"Oh." Lizzie stepped inside. She knew India was part of the British Empire, but she'd never met an Indian before. She bowed awkwardly. "Do you speak English?"

Hari smiled. "Yes. Do you?"

Lizzie flushed. "Of course." The elephant behind Hari shifted on the straw, and she backed away. "He's not gonna stomp on me, is he?"

Hari laughed. "No. And, by the way, he's a *she*."

"I ain't stayin' if you're gonna laugh at me!" Lizzie said. "How was I meant to know? They don't have bloomin' great elephants where I come from!"

Hari stroked the elephant's trunk gently. "I'm sorry." His brown eyes softened. "I know elephants make people nervous."

"They're just so big," Lizzie said, lifting her chin.

"This is Akula." Hari beckoned Lizzie closer. "Come and give her a stroke."

Lizzie had seen the elephant before when she was going for her bath. She was huge. As Lizzie eyed the enormous animal warily, another shape moved in the shadows on the other side of the tent. Lizzie stiffened as she realized it was a second elephant.

"That's Sashi," Hari told her. "They're very gentle. Come." He beckoned again. "Come stroke Akula on her trunk — that's her nose."

Reluctantly, Lizzie stepped forward and reached out a hand. She was determined not to tremble, but her fingers quivered as they neared Akula's trunk.

"Don't be afraid. She likes to be stroked," Hari reassured her.

Gently, Lizzie touched Akula's trunk. It felt dry and warm. Akula stood still while Lizzie ran her fingers over the rough hide.

"See?" Hari said. He reached up and scratched Akula behind her ear.

Akula curled the end of her trunk, and Lizzie saw its soft pink tip. *Imagine having a nose that long,* she thought.

Hari grinned as Akula lifted her trunk higher and sniffed Lizzie.

Lizzie forced herself not to run as the elephant ran the snuffling tip of her trunk over her. "Hello, Akula." She stroked her trunk. "I'm new here. I guess I smell funny."

Akula lifted her trunk higher and puffed air into Lizzie's face. Lizzie hopped backward in surprise.

"She likes you!" Hari laughed.

"Really?" Lizzie looked at him.

"Really." Hari picked up a short, stout stool and put it beside Akula's foreleg. "Come on, girl."

"What are you doing?" Lizzie asked.

"We have to file their toenails before the show," Hari explained.

"File their toenails?" Lizzie echoed. Hari couldn't be serious. "What with?"

Hari lifted a large iron file from the straw. "This." He tapped the back of Akula's leg. "Come on, girl."

Akula lifted her foreleg and placed it on the stool. Bending down, Hari began to file her huge toenails.

Lizzie watched, amazed, as the file sent a shower of dust onto the straw. Hari worked steadily and quietly. There was a calmness about him that put Lizzie at her ease. "How did you know the elephants made me nervous?" she asked.

"People often get cross when they're scared." Hari kept gently filing one nail after another. "Next leg, girl." He tapped Akula, and she swapped legs.

Lizzie crouched down in the straw and cupped her chin in her hands. Hari was a slender boy with smooth brown skin and the darkest eyes Lizzie had ever seen. His black hair curled softly at his neck as he worked.

"Do you want to try?" he asked suddenly.

Lizzie blinked. "I d-don't know."

Hari held the file out. Lizzie took it and approached Akula's huge foot. Tentatively, she gave one of the toenails a swish with the file. It slid over the nail.

"Harder," Hari encouraged.

Lizzie swished the file again, more firmly. This time dust showered from the nail. Akula swayed beside Lizzie but didn't move her foot.

"That's perfect," Hari murmured.

Lizzie began filing the nail where it hung over the edge of Akula's pad. She was concentrating so hard she barely felt Akula's trunk snuffling her back.

"There," she said at last, straightening and admiring her work. Akula's toenails were short and smooth. She gave the file back to Hari. "You'd better do the back ones," she said. "I don't know how to make her swap legs."

Lizzie sat back in the straw while Hari moved the stool and began filing the toenails on Akula's hind legs. Suddenly she realized how quiet it was here. Outside, the circus was bustling, but Hari was alone in the elephant tent. "Don't you get lonely with just the elephants for company?" Lizzie asked.

Hari shook his head. "I prefer it," he said, patting Akula's side. "Animals are easier to be around than people sometimes. They never hide what they're really feeling. You never have to guess."

"I s'pose," Lizzie said. She touched the bruise on her cheek — it had always been clear what Pa was feeling. Lizzie wondered suddenly about the Phantom. The show folk had been talking about him all day, shocked by the violent turn his crimes had suddenly taken. "What do you suppose the Phantom is feeling when he commits his crimes?"

Hari went on filing. "I think he's ashamed."

"Why?"

"Because he wears a mask. People do that when they're ashamed of themselves."

Lizzie remembered the ghoulish sketch in the newspaper. "Do you think it really is a mask?"

"It must be," Hari insisted. "That's no human face."

"Some people are saying he's *not* human."

"Oh, he's human all right," Hari argued. "*Very* human. That mask doesn't just cover his shame — it makes him feel bigger and better than he really is. Haven't you noticed how people often use clothes to make themselves look important?"

Lizzie pictured the rich folks on Oxford Street. They were always done up in silks and top hats, like they were more important than the beggars and tradesmen who had to wear what was needed rather than what they wanted.

"I hope they catch him soon," Hari said softly.

"So do I," Lizzie agreed.

"If he's turned violent, it means that robbery isn't thrilling enough anymore," Hari said. "If it's excitement he's after, he's going to get more and more dangerous."

Lizzie tucked her knees under her chin and hugged them close. "I hope not."

Hari stepped away from Akula and slid the file into his back pocket. He smiled suddenly, his white teeth bright in the dusky light. "Come on." He held out his hands, and Lizzie grabbed them and let him pull her up. "How would you like to sit on an elephant's back?"

Lizzie swallowed nervously. "I don't know."

"Here." Hari tapped Akula's leg and she lifted it. "Put your foot up here."

Surprising herself, Lizzie climbed onto Akula's knee.

"Up, Akula, up!" As Hari spoke, Akula wrapped her trunk around Lizzie's waist and hoisted her up into the air.

Lizzie gasped as Akula sat her gently down on her back. She stared down at Hari. He seemed a hundred feet away. "It's so high!" She wanted to laugh with exhilaration. She was sitting on top of an elephant!

"Lizzie?" Erin popped her head round the door.

"What are you doing up there?" Nora asked, following her sister into the tent.

"I'm being the Queen of Sheba," Lizzie said proudly.

"Come down!" Nora flapped her hands. "Malachy's bringing someone to meet you!"

"Who?" Lizzie turned onto her belly and let herself slide down Akula's side. She felt Erin and Nora's hands catch her and lower her gently onto the straw.

Malachy's voice sounded from the doorway. "I would like to present . . ."

Erin made a drumroll sound while Nora tooted like a trumpet through her hands.

". . . the *Great* Dru Boisset!" Malachy waved his arm with a flourish, and the boy from the poster came somersaulting through the doorway. Landing as nimbly as a cat, the boy threw out his arms and bowed.

Lizzie stared at him. She'd thought the artist might have exaggerated how good-looking he was, but no — he really was that handsome, his green eyes sparkling in the half-light.

"Are you one of the acrobats?" Lizzie asked. It was all she could think of to say.

"An acrobat?" The Great Dru Boisset lifted his hands in mock horror. *"Mais non!"*

Nora and Erin collapsed into giggles, and Malachy gave Dru a playful shove. "Stop showing off." He turned to Lizzie. "Dru works in the high-wire act."

"The high wire!" Lizzie felt dizzy just thinking about it. "With that lady on the penny-farthing bicycle?"

"She's my sister, Collette." Dru flung himself down onto a heap of straw. Erin and Nora curled up next to him, pulling Lizzie down beside them.

"Don't you get scared up there?" Lizzie asked. She couldn't imagine being that high off the ground.

Dru shook his head. In perfect English, with the slightest hint of a French accent, he said, "Up there is the only place I feel like *me*."

Lizzie glanced at Hari. "Like Hari with his elephants."

"And us on horseback!" Nora added.

Malachy sat down. "I feel happiest with my feet firmly on the ground." He tapped his club foot with his stick. "Even if one of them's firmer than the other."

"Join us, Hari!" Erin called. "I know we're not elephants, but we're nearly as nice."

Hari grinned and gave Akula a pat, then sat cross-legged beside Nora.

"Right." Erin leaned forward and stared at Lizzie, eyes bright. "We want to know all about you."

"Me?" Lizzie felt suddenly self-conscious.

"Of course!" Nora insisted. "You're the most exciting thing to happen here for ages!"

"I'm not exciting," Lizzie told them quickly.

"Of course you are," Dru argued. "You are a mystery, appearing from nowhere in the night."

"Where are you from, Lizzie?" Erin leaned closer.

"A place called Rat's Castle."

"Rat's Castle?" Nora wrinkled her nose. "That sounds horrible." She slapped her hands over her mouth. "Sorry, I didn't mean to sound rude!"

Lizzie shook her head. "You're right. It *is* horrible. It's stinky and mean and full of beggars and thieves and there's no one magic like you lot."

Malachy tipped his head to one side. "Is that why you ran away?"

Before Lizzie could answer, Hari's steady gaze fixed on her. "What about your family, Lizzie? Won't they miss you?"

Lizzie looked down. "My mother and brother are dead."

Hari's eyes grew round with sympathy. "My mother is dead too."

"So's mine," Malachy sighed.

Lizzie touched the bruise on her cheek. "And Pa . . ." she hesitated. "Pa's just . . . Pa."

"Oh, Lizzie!" Nora flung her arms around her. "You poor thing!"

"I'm not a poor thing! Look!" Lizzie shook her off. "Look where I am! I'm not poor at all."

* * *

Later, as the crowds faded and the circus grew quiet, Lizzie snuggled deep into her bunk beside Nora and Erin. The Sullivans snored and mumbled around her, tucked above and below like loaves in an oven. For the first time since Ma had died, Lizzie felt safe and warm. Smiling to herself, she closed her eyes. She was soon dreaming of high wires and elephants.

Swooping from a trapeze, Lizzie landed lightly on her feet in the elephant tent. Akula lifted her trunk to greet her but, as Lizzie reached out her hand to stroke the gentle creature, she vanished into darkness.

Lizzie spun around. Shadows swamped every corner.

"Akula?" Lizzie strained to see. "Hari?"

"Lizzie," a voice answered back.

"Who's there?" Lizzie tiptoed forward.

"Are you looking for me?" the voice asked.

Lizzie's heart quickened as she heard rasping breathing ahead. A face loomed from the shadows.

The Phantom!

Snarling, he lunged. His black cloak fluttered as he flew at her. He slammed into her, and she staggered backward. . . .

As she hit the ground, Lizzie woke with a gasp.

Nora moved beside her and sighed. Around her, the Sullivans still snored and mumbled in their sleep. Relieved, Lizzie let herself sink into the soft mattress, her heart slowing as she drifted back into sleep.

CHAPTER 5

The next morning, the hustle and bustle of the Sullivan family's caravan made it easy for Lizzie to forget her nightmare about the Phantom.

"Come on!" Erin tugged Lizzie out of the caravan while Nora raced behind.

"Why won't you just tell me what they're called?" Lizzie leaped over a rope as Erin swung her past the Lobster Boy's penny gaff.

"I will when we get there!" Erin said, dodging past the elephant tent.

Lizzie had been asking about the humpback horses over breakfast in the caravan. "Humpback horses!" Nora and Erin had burst into fits of giggles.

Patrick, shoveling in porridge at the far end of the table, had choked with laughter while Ma and Pa Sullivan exchanged smiles across Pa's newspaper.

"We'll get to the humpbacks in just a while." Erin skidded to a halt beside the horse pen.

Conor was brushing down his golden mare at the far side. "Don't be expecting me to brush Marigold and Daisy down for you again today," he told his sisters. "I've got to practice my somersaults. I've no time for grooming."

"I hear you," Erin hollered back. "We're just showing Lizzie the animals." She was ready with a sugar lump as her pony came trotting to meet her. "There you go, Marigold." She stood on the bottom rung of the fence and leaned over. Marigold whickered and nibbled it softly from her palm.

"Hello, Daisy." Nora climbed the rail beside them and took a sugar lump from her pocket as her pony nudged Marigold aside. "Here, Lizzie. You give it to her. Rest it on your palm and keep your thumb tucked in," she advised.

Lizzie held her hand out gingerly, thumb tucked in. She felt the pony's warm breath as it nuzzled her palm and softly took the sugar.

"Good girl, Daisy." Nora patted the pony's neck.

Lizzie looked around. "Where are the humpbacks?" she asked.

"They're called camels." A deep voice sounded from the pen beside them. Mario, the circus giant, was leaning over the fence. "Come say hello. I'm just about to feed them."

Lizzie clambered over the fence and jumped down beside Mario. "That's them!" She pointed excitedly at the two camels grazing on the far side of the pen. They looked even stranger in the sunshine, their brown pelts shaggy and their humps tufted and floppy at the top.

"Wait here." Mario held up a hand as Erin and Nora leaped down beside Lizzie. "Camels can be grumpy first thing in the morning, and when they're grumpy, they spit."

"Like Pa," Lizzie muttered.

Erin nudged her. "Conor's a champion spitter, so he is."

"He can spit the length of the circus ring," Nora boasted.

"Can you spit, Lizzie?" Erin asked.

Lizzie grinned. "I could knock a fly outta the air if I wanted." She left Nora and Erin exchanging impressed glances as she hurried after Mario. He was beckoning from beside the camels as they leaned down and munched hay from the pile he'd scattered at their feet.

"This is Sultan." Mario scratched the thick pelt of one of the camels. "And this is his partner Sabira."

Sabira lifted her head and blinked.

"Look at her eyelashes! They're so long." Lizzie pointed at the drooping hump. "And what's that for?"

"To store water in." Mario patted Sultan. "For long treks across the desert." He winked. "D'you want to see something better?"

"Better than camels?" Lizzie followed Mario out of the pen and past the show tent. Beyond the ropes, she could see the King of the Jungle's cage. A golden pelt stretched on a carpet of straw. "Is that Leo?" She raced to the pen and peered through the bars.

The lion lifted his wide head and shook out his mane.

"You've heard about him, then?" Mario crouched down beside her and stuck his fingers through the bars.

"So it's true he's old and got no teeth!" Lizzie said. The big cat was so handsome. "Poor ol' thing."

"He's had a good life," Mario assured her. "Been with Fitzy since he was a cub. Lost his teeth from too much cotton candy."

Leo leaned forward and licked Mario's fingers with a massive tongue.

"He's a pussycat!" Lizzie giggled.

Erin and Nora caught them up. "Are you still scared of Leo?" Nora teased.

Leo stretched out and flexed his claws. They were like butcher's hooks.

"I wouldn't get in a cage with him." Lizzie gazed at Leo. "Who does?"

"Fitzy," Erin crouched beside her. "He's Fitzy's act. He has Leo jumping through hoops every show. The crowd loves it. Leo acts all fierce, and then Fitzy acts fiercer."

"It's just a big game for them both," Nora said with a grin. "They're old friends."

"Come on." Erin jumped to her feet. "Let's leave Leo in peace and watch Dru practice."

"Lord, yes!" Lizzie hadn't seen the high wire act yet. She chased after Erin, tugging Nora by the hand. "Thanks, Mario!" she called over her shoulder.

They girls ducked into the show tent, where the smell of sawdust and canvas filled Lizzie's nose. She hadn't seen the show yet — she'd been too busy helping the performers — but she'd peeked inside the red-and-black striped tent on her way to fetch pegs for Mario yesterday. This was the first time she'd been inside, though.

Malachy was sitting on the brightly painted ledge that surrounded the wide stretch of sawdust. Clowns jumped and tumbled in the middle. Lizzie laughed as one pulled the hat of another down over his face. Water shot out of the top.

"Look!" Erin pointed at the roof.

Lizzie craned her neck and saw Dru waving from a platform high up on a fat tent pole. Arms stretched out, he stepped out onto a wire strung across the ring and walked across.

Lizzie swallowed. "What if he falls?"

"He'll die." A voice said from behind her, and Lizzie swung around. The girl in spangled tights she'd seen yesterday with the penny-farthing bicycle was standing behind them. It was Dru's sister, Collette.

Lizzie searched Collette's face. It was gaudy with makeup and pretty as a doll's. But no worry showed in her round blue eyes. *Doesn't she love her brother?* thought Lizzie.

Malachy leaned forward on his cane. "No one's ever died at Fitzy's circus," he told Lizzie. "And Pop says Dru can have a safety net if he wants."

"I wish he would." Nora clasped her hands together.

Erin sighed. "He says safety nets are for kids."

"But he's hardly more than a kid, ain't he?" Lizzie looked up, relieved, as Dru reached the far platform.

Collette shrugged. "He's old enough to earn his own living."

Dru was shimmying down the tent pole. He leaped the last few feet and raced across the ring. "Impressed?" he asked, stopping beside Lizzie.

Lizzie was about to answer when a figure caught her eye. Marching into the ring was a woman. At least, she was *dressed* like a woman. But a handsome beard covered her cheeks, and hair sprouted from her neck and arms as thickly as if she was wearing fur. She stopped beside a short fat clown, grabbed him by the lapels and kissed him hard.

"That's Ursula!" Erin said, following Lizzie's gaze. "The Bear Woman."

Lizzie stared. "Why's she kissing clowns?"

"That's her husband, Rice Pudding Pete," Nora said.

"Rice Pudding Pete?" Lizzie echoed.

Erin sat down beside Malachy. "He closes the act by falling into a vat of rice pudding."

Dru ducked in front of Lizzie, blocking her view. "My act? What did you think?"

Lizzie blinked into Dru's green eyes. "It was amazing! I could hardly breathe. How d'you keep your balance?"

Dru ran his fingers through his hair. "Practice."

Collette frowned at Ursula. "She should be in her booth with the other freaks, not in here with the *performers*."

Lizzie felt a surge of annoyance. *How dare she?* Anita's words rang in her mind. *People used to throw things at me, kick me . . . like I was no more than a dog.*

Before she could stop herself, Lizzie burst out with, "Who are you calling a freak?" She looked Collette up and down. "Standing there in your underwear! They're people, just like you an' me!"

Just then Lizzie saw Fitzy standing behind Collette. Oh, no! Was he going to be furious with her for shouting at one of the stars? She shut up quickly.

But Fitzy was smiling. "Well said, Lizzie. We're a family here at Fitzy's circus." He flashed a stern look at Collette. "We may bicker, but no one is more important than anyone else and we look after each other, right?"

Collette looked at him from under her lashes. "Right," she muttered sulkily.

"Go and get on with your practice." Fitzy shooed Collette away and fixed his gaze on Lizzie. "I've got a special job for you."

Lizzie straightened. Did someone need her to fix their stage or iron their costume? "I'm ready."

Fitzy smiled at her. "Good." He glanced down at her dress — the same shabby gray frock she'd been wearing since she'd arrived. "Erin!" he called over his shoulder. "You're about the same size as Lizzie. Can she borrow your Sunday dress?"

"Of course." Erin nodded. "Why? Is she going to church?"

"Not quite." Fitzy started to lead Lizzie out of the tent. "Madame Aurora needs an assistant."

★ ★ ★

As visitors started streaming toward the circus, Lizzie stood beside the Sullivans' caravan in Erin's Sunday best with her chestnut brown hair stiffly braided. She felt as trussed up as a Christmas goose.

"Mercy, Lizzie," Nora said with a giggle. She handed her Ma Sullivan's ivory-back mirror. The black taffeta made Lizzie look white as a ghost.

Lizzie scowled. "I look like I'm off to a funeral."

"You might as well be," Erin told her gravely.

Nora grasped her hand. "Be good," she warned. "Madame Aurora can be an awful banshee."

"She's a bit cranky," Fitzy explained as he led Lizzie toward Madame Aurora's tent. "But do as you're told, and you'll be right as rain. Just stand there and look mournful while she's doing her readings." He stopped outside a tent and lifted the flap. "She does palms and cards and the old crystal ball. You know the kind of thing. She just needs you looking sad and serious to help add a little solemnity to proceedings. Madame Aurora," he called inside, "your new assistant is here."

Lizzie peered into the shadows. Exotic perfume filled her nose. An oil lamp, turned low, barely lit the luxurious drapes that swathed the inside of the tent.

"Send her in." A sultry voice sounded in the dim light.

As Lizzie stepped inside, she could just barely make out a figure seated at a table. Madame Aurora stood up regally, shimmering with sequins and jingling with jewelery. A blood-red veil covered her face. She lifted it, and Lizzie saw the strong features of a handsome woman, caked with heavy makeup.

"Not much of a girl." Madame Aurora poked Lizzie's shoulder with a bony finger. The nail dug deep beneath Lizzie's shoulder bone.

Lizzie flinched but held her tongue. She wasn't going to risk losing her first proper job in the circus.

Madame Aurora lifted one of Lizzie's braids and let it fall from her fingers like a dead mouse. "Couldn't you find anyone more exotic?" she asked stonily. "This one looks like she's fresh from the workhouse."

Fitzy put his hand gently on Lizzie's shoulder. "She's a good worker, and she's bright. Her looks will improve once we've fed her up a bit."

Lizzie dug her nails into her palms. *Why do grown-ups have to be so rude? Like kids don't have proper feelings.*

Madame Aurora tossed her headscarf back and turned to her table. "I'll do what I can with her." She pointed to the doorway. "Stand there, girl."

"My name's Lizzie." Lizzie lifted her chin.

"While you're working here, you're called Roxanna." Madame Aurora sat down and gazed into the crystal ball sitting on her table, her ringed fingers fluttering around it. "Guide the client in, show them to their seat, then stand back and keep your mouth shut. I don't want them knowing you're a guttersnipe from the slums."

Lizzie flashed Fitzy a worried look as he hovered outside the doorway.

"You'll do fine." He glanced over his shoulder. "Here comes your first customer."

Madame Aurora quickly pulled her veil down over her face as Fitzy hurried away. A young woman was approaching the tent warily. Her eyes were red, and her nose was rosy from crying. Lizzie beckoned her in, and the young woman offered her a coin, but Madame Aurora's voice called out, smooth as honey, "I'll take your coin, dear. The spirits won't speak unless you cross my palm with silver."

Lizzie ushered the woman to the empty chair opposite Madame Aurora and then stepped back into the shadows. She watched as Madame Aurora pocketed the coin.

"Why have you come to seek guidance from the spirit world?" Madame Aurora's veil trembled.

You should know, Lizzie thought. *You're meant to be psychic.* She shuffled her feet.

Madame jerked her head in Lizzie's direction. "Stand still!" she hissed.

As Madame turned back toward her client, Lizzie stuck out her tongue. Madame Aurora didn't see; her gaze was fixed on the young woman who was now dabbing her nose with a handkerchief. "You seem troubled, my dear."

The woman nodded.

Well, that's obvious! Lizzie thought.

Madame stroked the air around her crystal ball. "I see heartache."

The woman sniffed and wrung her hanky between her fingers.

"Let me see." Madame Aurora gently lifted one of the woman's hands and turned her palm so it faced upward. Leaning over it she mumbled and shook her head. "You have known sorrow."

The woman sniffed again.

"Your love line is broken, see?" Madame Aurora pointed toward the woman's palm.

The woman looked closer. "I've been let down," she confessed.

"A man you trusted has abandoned you," the psychic continued.

As Madame Aurora spoke, the woman swallowed back a sob. "Archibald."

"He was not the man for you," Madame Aurora assured her. "Look." She ran a finger over the woman's palm. "Beyond the break, the line runs long and smooth. Another man waits, more trustworthy and with a faithful heart. You will find your true happiness with him."

Can she really tell that just by looking at her palm? Lizzie wondered.

The young woman's shoulders rose as though a great weight had been lifted from them. "Thank you!" The young woman stood up and began to back out. "Thank you so much."

Lizzie quickly stepped forward to pull the curtain aside. Another client was waiting outside — a man this time, his forehead furrowed. He hardly acknowledged Lizzie as she waved him toward the chair.

Madame Aurora looked him over, and Lizzie followed her gaze as it lingered on his frayed collar and the threadbare hat he rolled in his hands.

The psychic gazed into her crystal ball. "Financial worries weigh heavily on you." The man nodded.

Even I could tell that by just looking! Lizzie thought.

"But fortune awaits." Madame Aurora peered harder into her ball.

"Fortune?" The man sat forward in his chair, and Madame held out her palm.

The man reached into his pocket and handed her a coin at once. "What fortune?"

"Fortune beyond your wildest imaginings," Madame Aurora promised. "In business, your path is assured. I see water." She lifted her veil and peered even closer into the crystal. "Great oceans bearing great ships."

"Should I invest in shipping?" In the dim light, Lizzie could see the back of the man's neck flush with excitement.

"Your fortune will come from overseas." Madame Aurora's voice deepened.

She's just telling him what he wants to hear! Lizzie thought. She wanted to warn the man not to trust Madame Aurora's advice. But if she did, she'd lose her job; maybe even her place in the circus. She bit her lip and stayed quiet as Madame Aurora went on.

"Great wealth is within your reach; you need only wait and it will fall into your lap."

The man was fidgeting with excitement. 'Thank you, Madame Aurora!" He jumped to his feet and was out of the tent before Lizzie had time to lift the door.

"How can you get him all worked up like that?" Lizzie demanded.

Madame Aurora lifted her head. "I only tell what the spirits instruct," she murmured.

"Sure you do," Lizzie muttered as she lifted the flap for the next client.

★ ★ ★

"She makes it all up, I swear!" Lizzie paced back and forth beside Akula while Erin, Nora, Malachy, and Hari lounged in the hay. The last show had finished, and chores were done. Before long, Ma Sullivan would be shouting them back to the caravan for bed.

Lizzie grabbed an old sack and draped it over her head like a veil. "You are very troubled, my dear. . . ." Copying Madame Aurora's throaty whisper, Lizzie knelt beside Malachy and peered into his palm. "I see from your life line that you are young. But don't worry . . . you'll get older!" She grabbed Erin's hand next. "You are troubled, dear. You have to sleep in a caravan with four snoring brothers." She grasped Hari's hand. "I see in your love line that your next sweetheart will be an heiress! You will live in the best houses and eat only the best food."

As her friends hooted with laughter, Lizzie straightened. "But the best was the rich folks. She took longest with them. I expect she thought she was going to get an extra shilling. Mercy, did she ask them questions! As soon as a smart suit comes through the door, she's telling them they'll win big on the stock market and then asking them where their houses are and where they work. Do you know what she said?"

Lizzie put on the haughty voice of Madame Aurora again. "'Once I am certain of your geographical location, the spirits speak to me stronger.' And when they told her where they lived and talked about their job in some bank

or other and she'd um and ah and say, 'Of course. I feel it
now. An inheritance is coming your way,' or 'Your wife will
give you a son before the year is out to carry on your noble
line.'" Lizzie flopped down into the straw beside Erin. "I
thought she was gonna do real magic. But it's all make-
believe."

Erin rubbed her back. "That's the circus, Lizzie. It's all
a big illusion."

"But *Anita's* real," Lizzie pointed out.

Malachy shifted beside Hari. "She's about the only one
who is. The Pig-Faced Woman's an old bear in a dress with
a shaved face."

Lizzie gaped at him. "What about the mermaid?"

"Fake tail made out of walrus hide," Nora laughed.
"And Sid the Lobster Boy's never even seen the sea. He was
just born with his fingers and toes fused together."

Lizzie heart sank. "So they're just scamming like Pa?"

"They're just making the best of what God gave
them," Nora told her. "People like to see a show, so we
give them a show."

Erin nodded. "A good show is a sure way to take folks'
minds off their troubles."

"Madame Aurora certainly did that." Lizzie lay back
in the straw. "Not one person got bad news. They all left
thinking they was gonna fall in love or find a fortune."

Hari lowered his dark lashes. "Isn't that better?" he
said softly. "To believe that something wonderful's going

to happen. Isn't that better than always worrying about the future?"

"I guess." Lizzie shrugged. "And I s'pose, sometimes, she may be right. Though if she'd told me a week ago I'd be working in a circus, I'd never have believed her in a million years."

"If you can call it working," said Collette. She'd slipped in silently. Lizzie clenched her fists but kept her mouth shut. Collette gave a dazzling smile and clapped her hands. "You're summoned, boys and girls. Hurry up! To the main tent!"

"What for?" Lizzie was instantly suspicious.

"So my brother can show off his new trick, of course." Collette's smile never faltered. "You aren't going to keep him waiting, are you?"

The others leaped to their feet and scrambled out. Lizzie followed, not really wanting to go, but not quite knowing why. Dru was agile and clever, wasn't he? He couldn't be in any danger . . . so why was a tight knot of fear growing in her stomach?

"You mustn't mind Collette," Hari said as she caught up to the rest of the group.

"I don't," Lizzie snapped.

Inside the huge tent it was gloomy and full of shadows. By day it had been a jolly place, but now that the audience had all gone home it seemed sad. Lizzie's creepy feeling grew worse.

Dru was standing at one end of the high wire, grinning down at her. In his pale costume, he looked like a ghost up there in the dark.

"And now, for your delight and delectation," he called out, "I shall demonstrate a brand-new feat, one never before seen in this circus!"

Erin gasped and nudged her sister excitedly. Malachy watched, wide-eyed. They all seemed transfixed as Dru stepped out onto the wire, arms outstretched. One careful footstep followed another. The wire wobbled beneath his feet.

"Come down!" The words burst out of Lizzie's mouth before she could stop them. "It ain't safe!"

"Have no fear," Dru said, as if he were talking to an audience and not to Lizzie. "I've practiced this one for hours on the training wire."

He was nearly at the middle of the wire now. It bowed under his weight.

Lizzie's heart pounded like a big bass drum. She had to make Dru stop, somehow. "You tell him!" she told Collette, rounding on the startled girl. "Tell him not to do it!"

"My brother is a professional. You're insulting his talent," Collette said softly.

Now Lizzie's palms were aching. The feeling of horror was taking over her whole body. "Come down!" she yelled again. Dru's life depended on it. She didn't know how she knew. She just *knew*.

"You'd better hush up, Lizzie," Malachy whispered. "You might put him off with that yelling."

"Something bad's going to happen," Lizzie muttered. "I just *know* it."

High above, Dru bent his knees. "A roll of the drums, please!"

Erin and Nora began to hammer with their hands on the hollow wooden step, and Lizzie could only look on helplessly as Dru bent his knees again and flipped up into the air. The high wire twanged beneath his body as he turned a full backward somersault. Lizzie bit her knuckle.

Dru's feet came down on the wire. It wobbled madly. He swayed his body from side to side, struggling to keep his balance.

In the next moment, with a sickening snap, the wire broke loose at one end. Its whole length rippled as it fell, taking Dru with it.

He tumbled, arms flailing, down toward his death.

CHAPTER 6

With an acrobat's reflexes, Dru grabbed for the wire. He caught it and held tight as it swung down, bringing him with it like a huge pendulum.

Everyone rushed forward. They gathered below the tent pole as Dru, white-faced, inched his way down the wire. He dropped the last few feet and stood there trembling with shock.

"I'm all right," he said, waving away their anxious questions. "These things happen."

"Not in this circus they don't!" Collette burst out. "This was no accident. Someone sabotaged that wire!" She turned on Lizzie. "It was you, wasn't it? You meant that to happen to *me*!"

"I never!" Lizzie yelled.

"Oh, no? Then how did you know my brother was in danger, eh?"

"I . . ." The words stuck in Lizzie's throat. How could she possibly explain? "I just had a feeling."

Collette just snorted at that.

Lizzie turned around, desperate for backup, but Nora and Erin were looking at her with doubtful faces. Surely they couldn't think she was responsible!

But it was Hari who came to her rescue. "I think you should all look at this," he said quietly. He held up the end of the fallen high wire, which was frayed and discolored.

"Mildew," said Dru, shaking his head. "It must have been rotting through for weeks. Collette, how many times have I said we need a new rope?"

Lizzie folded her arms. "I'm waiting for an apology."

Collette stared at Lizzie as if she were suddenly afraid of her. "You stay away from me," she hissed. "You spooky little fr —"

She stopped herself just in time, but Lizzie knew what she'd been going to say. *Freak*. Then, without another word, Collette turned and ran from the tent.

"I'm sorry about my sister," Dru said, patting Lizzie's shoulder in a way that made her shiver all over. "She'll calm down. She's just upset."

"You were just worried about Dru, weren't you?" Nora said to her. "That's all it was. Just a wee fret. Got yourself all worked up."

"I s'pose," Lizzie said.

But deep inside, she knew it had been something more. And by the looks on their faces, the others clearly thought so too.

* * *

Early the next day, when Lizzie went to meet Madame
Aurora, the first thing that greeted her was a low groan
from inside the tent.

Pa used to sound like that, she thought to herself. After
a night of drinking, he'd spend the morning nursing his
aching head. It was best to be as quiet as you could around
adults with hangovers — she'd learned *that* the hard way.
Softly, she moved the curtain aside and looked in.

Madame Aurora was still wearing last night's makeup,
and her eyes looked sunken and bloodshot. Lizzie had
caught her in the act of swigging from a bottle. Their eyes
met.

"Morning!" Lizzie said brightly.

Madame Aurora hastily stuck the bottle under the
table, which was covered with a spread of tarot cards.
Before it vanished, Lizzie smelled the sharp, unmistakable
tang of gin.

"Draw that blasted curtain!" the fortune-teller snapped.
"Too much light angers the spirits!"

Lizzie knew that the spirits couldn't care less about
the light, but she understood that the bright sunshine was
probably hurting Madame Aurora's throbbing head. She
moved into the tent and let the curtain fall closed behind
her. There was no sense in making an enemy of her new
boss.

"Well, I'm stuck with you, so I'm going to make use of you," Madame Aurora said. "The customers will be lining up soon. When they do, I want you to keep your eyes and ears open."

"Open for what?" Lizzie asked.

"Anything I can use!" the woman said, rubbing her eyes. "Do I have to spell it out for you, girl?"

"To get a better connection with the spirits, and such?" Lizzie said carefully.

"Of course. The more I know about the client ahead of time, the more I'll be able to . . . help them," Madame Aurora said.

Lizzie nodded slowly. So that was her game, was it? She had to hang around outside the tent listening to anything the waiting customers might let slip, like their job or where they lived, or even what they were planning to ask about. Then she would quickly tell Madame Aurora, who could pretend that the *spirits* had told her.

"I can do that, easy," Lizzie boasted.

"You'd better," Madame Aurora said. "There's another job you need to do. Do you know what *ambience* means?"

"It's a carriage they take sick people off in."

"That's an *ambulance*, you stupid girl," Madame Aurora snapped. "*Ambience* means an atmosphere. Creating mysterious ambience helps the client to believe."

Lizzie nodded. That must be what all the decoration inside the tent was for. Just more show, more illusion.

"I need you to help create ambience, understand? If I say something like 'Spirits, show your presence!' then you knock on the table or mess about with the lamps. Make 'em go low and flickery, that's always a good one."

"But don't get caught doing it," Lizzie added, starting to catch on.

Madame Aurora raised an eyebrow. Her makeup cracked like old plaster. "You're catching on quick. You might be more useful than I thought. Here, sit down." She stood, and made Lizzie sit down in her seat. Madame Aurora's breath stank of gin. "Communicating with the spirits takes a lot out of me," she explained. "I need to have a little nap now and again."

"I bet you do," Lizzie muttered.

"What was that?"

"Nothing," Lizzie said quickly.

Madame Aurora began to unwrap the veils and shawls from around herself and drape them on Lizzie. They smelled like old sweat and gin. Lizzie wrinkled her nose but said nothing. This was the only job she had, and she couldn't afford to lose it.

"While I'm resting, you'll have to cover for me," Madame Aurora told her. "Nobody will know it's not the real Madame Aurora under these wraps."

"What am I meant to tell them?" Lizzie protested.

"Hold your horses a moment. There! Now you look the part. Can you do the voice?"

Lizzie coughed. "You are troubled, dear," she said, just as she had the night before.

"Close enough. Now, take my hand as if I was the client. That big line down the middle of my palm is the life line."

"Got it," Lizzie said.

"Run your middle finger down the life line. Gently!"

"Like this?"

"That's it," Madame Aurora said.

Lizzie frowned. "That's funny."

"What? What's going on?"

"I can see something," Lizzie said breathlessly. "Pictures in my head."

"No, don't sound surprised!" Madame Aurora snapped at her. "You're supposed to be a psychic! And remember to do the voice. Start with something like 'the mists are parting. . . .'"

"No, I really *can* see something," Lizzie said. An image was forming in her mind, right behind her eyes, as if a magic lantern was shining it there. It was blurred, like a watercolor painting left out in the rain, but she could still make it out.

A boy, making a pile of sticks to burn a broken doll on. And a little girl, crying.

"It's a doll funeral," Lizzie said.

Madame Aurora nearly jerked her hand right out of Lizzie's grip. "What?"

"The doll's broken, and the boy wants to burn it, but the girl don't want him to."

"Amelia," Madame Aurora whispered, looking shocked. "How on earth . . ."

"Now there's something else." Lizzie moved her finger further down Madame Aurora's life line. "The picture's not quite so blurry this time. It's that girl again. But she's older. About sixteen? Wearing a bonnet. In a room, in a house. She's tying up a stack of letters with a big pink ribbon. And she's happy."

"Happy," Madame Aurora echoed.

Lizzie gulped and blushed a little. "I think they're love letters."

Madame Aurora opened her mouth and shut it again.

"Now she's on a stage, singing a song. The pictures are getting clearer! She's older now. She's trying her best, but they're booing her, poor thing." Lizzie suddenly realized who it was in the visions. "She looks like *you*!"

"What song?" Madame Aurora demanded. "What song, you little wretch?"

Lizzie strained to make it out. "'It was only a violet, plucked from my poor mother's grave . . .'"

Madame Aurora gasped. "How dare you? You ungrateful, prying —"

"Now I can see you, just like you are today. It's not blurry at all. It's so clear, it's like looking right at you! And there's bright light . . . you've got your robes on, in this here tent, and you're talking to a bloke. A posh-looking gent—"

What Lizzie saw next shut her up quickly. In her vision, Madame Aurora was quite clearly stealing from her client. Lizzie watched her reach across, lift a pocketwatch from the client's jacket, and slip it into her own. Then the vision vanished.

Madame Aurora snatched back her hand, and before Lizzie could say another word, she pulled her up by her shoulders, tore the veils and robes off her, and shoved her out of the tent.

"Who do you think you are, eh?" Aurora screeched from the doorway. "I'm the fortune-teller in this show, not you!" Then she bent over, clutching her head and wincing. "I'm going for a nap."

"What about the clients?" Lizzie protested.

"Forget the stupid clients! And forget you too. Get out of my sight! You're finished here, do you hear me? Finished!"

CHAPTER 7

Much later, after night had fallen, Lizzie made her way across the circus camp. Madame Aurora's angry words were still ringing in her ears. Above the London rooftops the stars were out, brilliant as sequins against the black velvet sky. They reminded Lizzie of the zodiac signs she'd seen on the drapes in Madame Aurora's tent — a swirl of fantastic beasts and mythical figures.

"Load of rubbish," she muttered. "They're just stars. People shouldn't go making up shapes that ain't there."

Lizzie knocked on the door of the Fitzgerald trailer, the largest of them all, and Malachy called from inside, "Come in, Lizzie! I think we can squeeze in one more."

Inside, the caravan was full of mementos — battered top hats, old canes, brightly colored juggling clubs. Even the walls were covered with playbills and pictures of past performances. Lizzie hesitated, wondering where on earth she could sit.

"Over here!" Nora called from where she sat cross-legged on the bed below the window. "We'll be snug as sausages."

Lizzie shuffled past Dru, Hari, and Erin, who were crowded around a low table playing cards. Piles of peanuts were changing hands instead of money.

"Take off those batts before you climb on the bed," Malachy warned her.

"He means your shoes," Nora said, laughing in response to Lizzie's blank look. "You'd better learn more circus lingo if you're going to be part of this troupe!"

Lizzie pulled her shoes off and sat down next to Nora. The bed was covered with a rainbow-colored patchwork quilt and heaped with pillows. A light rain began to rattle against the window, making Lizzie feel all cozy in this private world — it would hurt to have to leave.

"Won't do me much good to learn your ways if I'm getting thrown out on my ear tomorrow," Lizzie muttered.

Nora stared at her. "Who told you that?"

"Madame Aurora," Lizzie said. "Who'd you think?"

"Oh, don't let that woman scare you," Nora said. "It's just the gin talking. She's crazy for it."

"So I can stay? I don't have to go?" Lizzie asked hopefully.

Malachy looked up from his card game. "Of course you can stay. Why wouldn't you? Lizzie, you're as white as a sheet! What's this all about?"

The card game was instantly forgotten as they all crowded around her. Lizzie swallowed. "I—I don't think I should say."

"What did that old hag say to you?" Erin demanded.

"I didn't mean to do it!" Lizzie burst out. "I just saw things! The moment I touched her stupid old life line!"

It all came pouring out. Lizzie told them everything that had happened. As she described the visions, Erin and Nora listened open-mouthed. Malachy paid close attention, and Dru folded his arms and said nothing.

But Hari . . . Hari didn't even seem surprised. "I think you have a gift, Lizzie," he said quietly.

"Get out of here!" Lizzie protested. "I do not."

"In India, we have holy men who are supposed to have wonderful powers," Hari said. "They can levitate, read minds, and even walk on hot coals. Perhaps . . ."

Lizzie was having none of it. "I'm not from India! I'm from Rat's Castle!"

"Sounds like you saw Aurora's life story," Malachy said. "Pretty miserable life too."

"Lizzie saw her past," Hari agreed. "But I wonder . . . you say the visions become clearer the closer you came to the present day?"

"Yes." Lizzie nodded.

"So the blurrier a vision is, the further in the past it is," Hari said. "Tell me, was there a vision that was clearer than clear? Shining bright?"

"Yes! How did you know?" Lizzie asked.

"Just a guess," Hari said. "If you saw her past, maybe you saw her future too. That's how I'd expect it to look."

Nora gripped her arm excitedly. "The *future*? What did you see?"

"It was her, in the tent, like she is now," Lizzie said. "She had a rich man in there. She was stealing his watch."

Dru gave a low whistle, and Erin and Nora exchanged glances.

"I didn't mean to see it!" Lizzie protested. "I couldn't help it!"

Malachy rubbed his chin. "Old Aurora, a thief? I wouldn't be surprised if that was true."

That took Lizzie by surprise. "Really?"

"Come on, have you seen how much gin she goes through? More than she could afford on a fortune-teller's wages, I bet."

"She's a proper drunk," Erin agreed, nodding.

"Gets into trouble all the time when she's been drinking," said Nora. "Remember the fight she had with the Amazon Queen?"

"Savage, it was! Scratching and hair pulling! Rolling in the straw!"

"If Anita hadn't knocked her cold with that tent peg, she'd have killed someone!" Nora laughed.

Lizzie didn't think it was funny. She was beginning to realize she'd made a dangerous enemy. If a drunken Madame Aurora could attack the huge Amazon Queen, then what chance did a skinny young girl have? "Forget it," she mumbled. "It must have been my imagination."

"And when the rope broke, and I fell? Was that your imagination too?" Dru asked, speaking for the first time.

"She's got the second sight," Erin said, totally sure. "That proves it. Here. Do me next."

Lizzie squirmed away from Erin's offered hand. "I don't believe in none of that stuff."

Dru shrugged. "Seeing is believing."

Lizzie had never believed in anything supernatural — she wasn't even afraid of ghosts, not like other children she knew. After all, Pa's fists were more scary than any ghost could be. And now this.

"But this circus stuff ain't real," she said desperately. "It's all just for show."

"Some of it is," Malachy told her. "But it's a big old world, Lizzie. There are a lot of strange things in it that you can't easily explain."

"S'pose you'd know," Lizzie said sullenly.

Malachy grinned. "We've been to a lot of places, us circus folk. Seen things that would turn your hair white. You're going to have to open your mind if you're going to stay with us."

It was a lot to take in. Lizzie looked down at her own open hands, wondering if she really did have the power to see into people's lives. Deep inside she suddenly believed she did. Whether she liked it or not, there wasn't any other explanation. All through her life, she'd had premonitions. She'd dreamed of her mother's death, and her brother's, but she'd thought it was just coincidence — after all, people died all the time in Rat's Castle.

The only question now was what she should do with her powers. Well, they could help make money, for a start. If she could tell people about their past the way she had with Madame Aurora, they'd be more likely to part with their cash. She might even pick up on some forgotten happy times that customers would be glad to be reminded of.

"Looking into the past is harmless enough, I reckon," Lizzie said. "But do you really think I can see into the future?"

"Like when you saw Aurora stealing?" Malachy rested his chin on his fist. "That vision was clearer than the rest, right?"

"All bright and shiny." Lizzie nodded.

"So if that *was* the future, then perhaps she hasn't stolen anything yet. . . ." A faraway look came over Malachy's face. Suddenly, he jumped to his feet. "Lizzie, I've got it! We can't change the past, but we *can* change the future."

"What are you going on about?"

"Maybe you've been given visions so that you can stop bad things happening!"

"How?" Lizzie asked, flabbergasted.

"Think about it. If something bad hasn't happened yet, maybe it doesn't have to happen at all," Malachy said.

"If you knew when and where a robbery was going to happen," Hari added excitedly, "you could get there first and stop it!"

"You could be a hero!" Erin said.

For once, Lizzie was completely lost for words.

★ ★ ★

The next morning, Lizzie was ready for work bright and early. She looked at herself in one of the carnival mirrors. Dressed in the dark, formal clothing she'd borrowed, she looked like a mourner at her own funeral. She sighed. Time to go face Madame Aurora's wrath.

But the moment Lizzie headed for the fortune-teller's tent, she started to attract attention. A clown smiled through a beard of shaving foam and waved. Women whispered behind their hands, and an old man blew out a cloud of pipe smoke and nodded knowingly.

Lizzie picked up speed, but that only made people more excited. Now people were standing up, abandoning half-eaten breakfasts, stowing away borrowed newspapers. She heard someone call out, "There she is!"

Lizzie spotted Nora's red hair and strode across to her.

"Good morning!" Nora said with a smile that spoke volumes.

"Did you and Erin tell everyone about me having visions?" Lizzie demanded.

"Oh, we might have let it slip," Nora said breezily. "Now would you look at that, you've got customers already."

Lizzie spun around. Sure enough, people were heading directly for her. A group of eight or nine circus folk quickly gathered around her, talking excitedly.

A lean, brown-skinned man stepped forward first. It was Zezete, the man she had met taking Akula the elephant for her bath. "My nephew Hari tells me you have a gift," he said.

"Hari too?" Lizzie rounded on Nora. "So the whole lot of you have been telling tales about me, have you?"

"My dear girl, it is nothing to be ashamed of!" Zezete smiled at her. "Such gifts are given for a reason, always."

Lizzie shuffled her feet. "I don't want it."

"Why ever not?" Zezete asked.

Lizzie lowered her eyes. "I'll just get called a freak."

"But we are all freaks at Fitzy's circus," said Zezete with a wink. "You will fit right in."

Lizzie couldn't help but smile at that.

"So, madam, would you do me the honor of reading my palm?" Zezete asked.

Lizzie took a deep breath. "All right." She took his warm hand in hers, and the gathered crowd looked on eagerly. She found the life line. It was deep, like a weathered canyon carved through rock. The moment she put her finger to the line, visions began to appear in her mind. She saw a blazing sun, men wearing turbans, women with brightly colored cloth wrapped around them, and cows wandering down the middle of a busy road.

"I can see a town, but it's not in England. There's crowds of people, and cows in the street," Lizzie began.

"India," Zezete said confidently.

Lizzie gasped at the colors she saw before her — red and blue banners, gleaming gold on temple roofs, bright powder paint exploding like bombs in the midst of a joyous festival.

"There's a celebration," she said. "People chucking paint everywhere."

"Yes, yes!" Zezete said excitedly. "Holi, the festival of colors. Excellent. Very good. Go on."

"You're a little boy, and some old man is touching your head," Lizzie continued. "He looks holy."

"Swami Samarth," Zezete told the onlookers. "I was three! I had colic. My mother took me for a blessing."

"Now you're eating a cake with loads of layers."

Zezete groaned and licked his lips. "Bebinca."

Lizzie wondered how long it had been since Zezete had tasted any. The young boy in her vision was savoring every mouthful, and the vision was so intense that she could smell the sweetness of it. Her mouth began to water.

Suddenly the vision vanished, replaced by another. Zezete was a man now, still eating bebinca. He smiled at the beautiful woman who had brought it to him. Lizzie echoed what the woman said: "Happy birthday, my little squirrel."

Zezete began to tremble over his whole body. He whispered something in Hindi that Lizzie couldn't understand. "My Lakshmi," he begged. "Tell me more."

But the vision had faded. "I can't," Lizzie said helplessly.

"But you saw her! My wife. She always called me her little squirrel!" Zezete's face became solemn. "I will pay. Whatever you ask. Just give me more."

"Money won't help," Lizzie said. "I don't choose what I see. It just happens."

Zezete closed his eyes. "Very well. You must speak as you see."

Lizzie tried to focus again. Suddenly, just as had happened with Aurora, she saw a clear vision. "I see you in your trailer. You're looking in your traveling trunk, fishing around by some old boots. A ring's on a chain around your neck. Now you're standing up, but the chain's caught. The ring's fallen into the trunk."

Zezete sprang to his feet, eyes wide. "Thank you!" he said. Without warning, he kissed her on both cheeks and rushed off.

After that, everyone wanted their palm read. Lizzie had to make them all line up. She was in the middle of reading the palm of a Dutch acrobat named Erik when a shout of joy rang out from Zezete's caravan.

"So you're sure I don't have consumption?" Erik asked.

"How could you go on to have grandchildren if you have consumption?" Lizzie said. "I saw you with them. It was Christmas, and you were an old man! The only thing wrong with you now is a spot of hay fever. 'Scuse me a moment."

Lizzie turned to see Zezete sprinting toward her. He held up a golden ring that caught the light. "Lakshmi's wedding ring," he said through tears. "I lost it weeks ago, when the circus was in Cambridge. I thought it was gone forever."

Zezete grabbed Lizzie's arm and held it up as if she were a boxing champion. "Listen, all of you!" he declared. "This girl is *echt*, kosher, the genuine article! My mind-reading is only stagecraft, but she is a *bona fide* psychic!"

"What is this?" Madame Aurora suddenly screeched. The crowd parted, revealing the fortune-teller barreling toward Lizzie. "Shove off, all of you!" she told the onlookers. "This brat works for me, and don't you forget it!"

As the crowd dispersed, Aurora bent down low and whispered in Lizzie's ear. "Last chance. If you don't stop stealing my limelight, I'll get you fired — or worse."

"Worse?" Lizzie repeated.

Aurora grinned, showing her yellow teeth. "I can do magic too, you know. I can make nasty little girls disappear. Never to be seen again."

CHAPTER 8

Lizzie barely slept that night. All day she'd worked hard in the mystic tent, eavesdropping on the customers and fiddling with the lamp like Madame Aurora wanted, while the terrifying threat hung in the air between them.

"Never to be seen again . . ."

Lizzie shuddered and rolled over. Visions rose like smoke in her mind, keeping her from sleep. Aurora, grinning like a skull. A gleaming knife. The masked Phantom, laughing.

She woke up the next day, rolled groggily out of bed, and went to join the Sullivans for breakfast. Erin snatched her porridge away when it looked like Lizzie was about to pass out into it.

"Shall I fetch a bucket of water and chuck it over you?" Erin suggested. "Might wake you up."

"My legs ache," Lizzie moaned, rubbing her calf.

"That's because that old witch makes you stand in one place all day." Nora said.

Mr. Sullivan checked his watch. "You'd best be getting to work, Lizzie. She'll have a fit if you're late."

But when Lizzie arrived at the fortune-teller's tent, she found it empty. She hastily lit the lamp, set some incense burning, and tidied up as best she could, hoping it would improve Aurora's mood if she found the place ready for her.

Ten more minutes passed. Still no sign of Aurora.

Lizzie poked her head out of the tent and saw the first customers of the day waiting patiently in line. She bit her knuckles anxiously. It was bad for business to leave customers waiting. She could do the readings herself, of course, but Madame Aurora wouldn't like that, would she?

She paced back and forth, lit more incense, polished the crystal ball, straightened the tarot cards. Outside she heard someone mutter, "We can't expect these circus folk to turn up on time, can we?" Polite laughter followed.

This was just confirming all their prejudices about circus people. Lizzie snuck another peek outside. The line had grown to seven or eight people now. The gentleman at the back was frowning and looking at his pocketwatch.

Lizzie's blood turned to ice on the spot. It was the man from her vision. And that was the very watch she'd seen Aurora steal!

Just then, Madame Aurora barged into the tent, red-eyed and haggard. Ignoring Lizzie completely, she rummaged around under the table and came up empty-handed. "I was sure there was one more bottle . . . right, Roxanna. Let the first customer in."

Lizzie opened up the tent flap, feeling like she was trapped on a runaway train. Her vision was becoming a reality, and there was nothing she could do to stop it.

"About time," a gentleman muttered. He ducked past her first, wincing as he did so. "You'd better be good!"

Lizzie couldn't possibly get away now. She stood, her legs aching and her heart pounding, as Madame Aurora bluffed her way through the reading. "You are troubled, dear . . ." she began.

Lizzie cringed as the hungover fortune-teller mumbled her nonsense. It was a clumsy, half-hearted performance even by her usual standards.

The customer wasn't impressed, Lizzie could tell. She thought he might even demand his money back. She had to do something. Why had the man flinched in pain when he entered the tent? She glanced at his shoes. The left one was scuffed and worn down the side, as if he'd been favoring it. So, he had a bad leg. Maybe a war wound. She caught Aurora's eye and quickly mimed firing a gun, then slapped her leg.

"I see fighting in your past," Aurora said instantly. "A war wound, in the arm, *no*, in the leg. A brave soldier, who does not boast of his deeds . . ."

That made the man sit up and pay attention. *Nothing like flattery to win them over*, Lizzie thought sourly.

By the time he left the man was smiling, proud of himself. Lizzie had to get out. "Shall I pop out and have a look over the others, then?"

"Of course!" Aurora snapped. "You should have done that anyway."

Outside, Lizzie glanced at the line of customers. Her stomach lurched to see the man with the watch was even closer to the front now. Some of the others must have grown tired of waiting and left.

It looked like her vision was about to come true. She had to tell someone. But if she left her post, Aurora would have her fired for sure. She'd be risking everything.

Lizzie made her mind up. She sprinted off to find Malachy and Nora. "It's him," she gasped when she found them. "The gent with the watch! When he goes in that tent, she's going to nick it off him!"

"I knew you had second sight!" Nora said. "Didn't I say?"

Lizzie's palms were clammy. She hopped up and down on the spot. "But I dunno what to do!"

"I'll tell you what we're going to do," said Malachy. "We're going to catch her red-handed. Come on!"

When they arrived at the tent, the line had shrunk even more. The gentleman with the watch was at the very front.

Malachy took up position outside the tent while Lizzie slipped inside. Aurora was in the middle of a reading. The pudding-faced old woman across from her was nodding at her every word. Aurora caught Lizzie's eye, and the look she gave her was pure poison. Lizzie gulped and threw a fistful of incense on the hot coals. Billowing clouds of smoke filled the tent.

"I see many grandchildren in your future," Aurora went on. Behind her, the tent fabric twitched. Lizzie held her breath.

Nora came crawling in under the edge of the tent. The thick curtain of smoke almost hid her completely. Neither Aurora nor her client seemed to have noticed, and Lizzie watched with her heart in her mouth as Nora quickly ducked behind the cabinet holding Aurora's mystic props. When she was out of sight, Lizzie let out the breath she'd been holding.

The old woman stood up to go, thanking Aurora again and again. Impatiently, Aurora ushered her out and beckoned the gentleman from Lizzie's vision in. He sat down opposite her. "I've never consulted a fortune-teller before," he said anxiously.

"You have chosen wisely," Madame Aurora said in a husky voice. "The spirits have a special message for you."

"They . . . they do?" the man stuttered.

"Roxanna!" Aurora clapped her hands. "Bring me the crystal!"

Lizzie's hands shook as she went to lift the heavy crystal ball from its place in the mystic cabinet.

Nora's face peeped out from her hiding place, and she mouthed the words, *Is this him?*

Lizzie gave a quick nod and turned away. The crystal ball began to slip through her sweaty hands. She hastily set it on the table.

"I must enter a state of mystic trance," Madame Aurora proclaimed.

"Gosh," said the young man. "Right-o. Jolly good."

Madame Aurora began to rock back and forth. She gave a long, low groan like a sick horse, then rolled her eyes back into her head so that only the whites were showing. "Spirits! I call to you! Come forth from your shadow realm!"

The gentleman sat stiffly in his seat, watching in amazement.

"Give some sign of your presence!" Aurora said through bared teeth.

Lizzie wasn't the least bit impressed. She had seen this routine a dozen times before.

Madame Aurora groaned louder. "Spirits! Do not delay!"

Suddenly, Lizzie remembered she was supposed to flicker the lamp at this bit. The gentleman almost jumped out of his seat when the light dimmed. "Good lord," he murmured.

"The spirits bid you welcome, son of a noble line." That was one of Aurora's old favorite phrases to use. If the customer was high-born, they were flattered; if they were common, they were amazed to think their ancestors might have been blue bloods. Either way, it was a winner.

The gentleman looked helplessly to Lizzie. "What do I say?" he whispered.

"Lean forward," Aurora boomed before Lizzie could speak. "Gaze deep into the crystal. Only then can the message be given!"

He did as he was told, excitement all over his face. And the moment his waistcoat pocket came close enough, Aurora's hand moved like a striking snake. She wrapped her fingers around the watch, pulled it out, and tucked it into her own pocket.

"Malachy!" Lizzie yelled at the top of her voice. "Now!"

The poor gentleman jumped out of his chair with shock as Malachy pulled the tent flap back, letting in brilliant sunshine. A man was standing there in silhouette, arms folded. It was Fitzy himself!

"What's going on?" the customer cried, shielding his eyes.

"I'm afraid we're going to have to stop the reading," Fitzy said.

"But . . . but . . . the spirits . . ." the young man stuttered in total confusion.

"Never mind the spirits, my good sir," said Fitzy, taking his arm. "If you'd care to wait over here — *all* the way over here — that's it, so sorry for the inconvenience. I do hope you'll accept these free tickets for tomorrow's performance." He quickly ushered the man out of the fortune-teller's tent and away through the circus, talking all the while.

Madame Aurora was on her feet, but Malachy stepped into the doorway, blocking her path. "You're not going anywhere," he warned.

"What's this all about, Malachy my love?" she asked with a sickly smile.

Fitzy returned. "I'm hoping it's nothing," he said. "Well, Lizzie?"

"She stole his watch," Lizzie said boldly. "It's in her pocket. I saw the whole thing!"

"You're a rotten little liar," Aurora snapped. "You didn't see *nothing*!"

Right then, Nora sprang out from behind the cabinet, and Madame Aurora gave a satisfying yelp of total surprise. Lizzie grinned at her friend's perfect sense of showmanship.

"I saw it too, Fitzy," Nora said. "Lizzie's telling the truth."

With a weary sigh, Fitzy held out his hand. "Come on, Aurora. Let's have it."

Trembling, Aurora drew the watch out of her pocket. "I couldn't help myself," she said. "It was the spirits — they drove me to do it."

"The only spirit driving you is gin," Fitzy said angrily. "Nora, run and give the gentleman his watch back."

"Right you are!" Nora said.

"Tell him you found it on the ground and he must have dropped it. Enough of the public think we're thieves without us making it worse."

Aurora fell on her knees and clutched at Fitzy's trousers. "Don't call the police, Fitz," she begged. "I can't go to prison, not at my age."

"Save it, Aurora," Fitzy said. "Malachy, go fetch Joey and Bungo."

"Yes, Pop!" With a smart salute, Malachy darted off.

Aurora wailed and beat her fists on the dusty ground. "Please! You don't have to do this. I've been with you so long!"

Fitzy stood, hands on hips. "So give me another option."

"Let me go. I'll leave the circus and never come back, I swear!"

Fitzy pondered this. "All right. But no second chances this time, Aurora. You're out for good."

"Thank you, thank you!" Aurora struggled to her feet, tugged her mystic robes off, and flung them on the ground. "I'll just pop to my caravan, fetch a few things, then I'll be on my way —"

"You will leave *now*," Fitzy commanded in a tone that made Lizzie shiver.

Malachy arrived, followed by two huge circus hands. One was bald with a walrus mustache, the other shaggy and bearded like a mountain man.

Fitzy nodded to Aurora and jerked his head toward the exit. Bungo and Joey instantly understood. They reached for Aurora, but she was already backing away from them, retreating toward the main gate like a vampire being driven into its crypt. Ignoring her shrieks, they grabbed her by the arms and began to drag her off.

"You did this to me!" Aurora screamed at the top of her voice. "You! Lizzie Brown!" And she let fly a string of language so foul that Nora came up behind Lizzie and covered her ears.

"Get her off my site," Fitzy said in disgust.

"You better sleep with one eye open, Lizzie Brown!" Aurora screamed as she was dragged away. "You'll never be safe in London again! I'll get you! I got connections! I'm *somebody!*"

"She's just a drunken old witch," Nora said firmly.

But Lizzie's heart still thumped hard in her chest with every angry scream.

"You're dead meat!" came the fading cries. "Dead meat!"

Fitzy tucked his thumbs through his braces and gave Lizzie a broad smile, as if nothing unusual had happened at all. "Word travels fast in a circus," he said. "I've heard you've turned out to be a genuine psychic."

"That's right," Lizzie said. No sense in denying it *now*, was there?

Fitzy bent his knees, dropping down to Lizzie's level. "I seem to find myself in need of a fortune-teller. I don't suppose, by any chance, you'd be interested in filling the position?"

Lizzie gaped at him. "Who, me? I mean . . . yes! Yes, I would!"

"That's that, then." Fitzy smacked dust off his hands and peered up at the signage on the tent, gold letters on a midnight blue background. "Oh, dear. This won't do at all. 'Madame Aurora' is out of date now."

"I'll get Dawson to paint it up fresh, Pop," Malachy said.

Fitzy nodded. "I want it done by noon today. Now, what to write . . ." With his finger Fitzy traced the arch the new words would follow, speaking his thoughts aloud. "'The Magnificent Lizzie Brown,'" he declared. "There. How's that sound to you, Lizzie?"

"Fantastic," Lizzie said. "Absolutely blooming fantastic."

CHAPTER 9

Lizzie hadn't realized taking Madame Aurora's job would mean taking her caravan too.

Pa Sullivan had pointed that out to her over tea. "Now we don't mind having you bunk down with us in here," he added, "but that trailer's yours by right, and you need to lay your claim to it before some other fella does."

So Lizzie, Erin, Nora, and Dru had gone racing over to the black, peeling caravan sitting in the far corner of the field. Someone had once painted mystic symbols on the outside — a star, a moon, and a cross-eyed cat — but the paint had almost completely flaked off. It smelled musty, like an old, unopened room.

"It's enormous!" Lizzie said, climbing inside.

"It's ancient, is what it is." Nora looked around. "Ugh. Look at the mess Aurora's left it in. Even the spider webs are covered with dust!"

"I love it," Lizzie said firmly. "It's mine now. I'm going to look after it."

Nora spat on her palms and rubbed them together. "Well, you'll not be sleeping in it in this state! Let's make a home of it."

They made a bonfire of Aurora's old pillows and bedding, emptied out the cupboards and drawers, and borrowed a broom to sweep the dust out. Dru made a face when he found a grimy, old petticoat under the mattress. It went straight on the fire.

By the time the sun set, the caravan was an empty shell, smoked out with incense from the fortune-telling tent. A quick ask-around netted them enough fresh blankets and pillows to make it comfortable, just in time for the circus to break down the camp.

For the rest of the evening, there was nonstop work. Tents had to be taken down, canvas folded away, poles dismantled, stalls packed up — and all of it had to be done the right way, with no carelessness or corner-cutting. There was no room for someone who didn't help in Fitzy's circus. Lizzie found plenty to do, carrying stacked-up stakes and looping up ropes into neat piles. It was exhausting, but it felt good to be pitching in.

Now the stars were out, and the circus was on the move, heading across the sleeping city toward Tower Hamlets for their next stop. The long convoy of caravans and trailers moved slowly, with most of the circus folk sleeping while the drivers steered them through the night.

Lizzie, Erin, Nora, and Dru sprawled happily in Lizzie's jolting caravan, bone-weary but still too excited for sleep. The sound of Big Ben tolling rang out across the river and the rooftops.

"One in the morning!" Nora yawned. "Even the owls have gone to bed."

"Please, Lizzie," Dru begged, holding his palm out, "I want to know my future!"

Nora laughed. "Are you still pestering her?"

"Please!" Dru said again.

"Not a chance," Lizzie said, smirking.

"Give it up, Dru," said Erin.

Dru pouted. "So unfair. All day she reads the palms of *les étrangers!* But I ask her to read mine, as *un ami*, and she says no!"

"It's a lady's right to refuse," Lizzie said primly.

"Perhaps you are afraid of what you may see." Dru unbuttoned his shirt and leaned back on the pillows, as if he was trying to play the part of an Arab sheikh. "'What if he does not love me like I love him?' you are thinking. 'I would die.'" Dru put his hand theatrically to his forehead.

"You must have hit your head when you fell off that high wire," Lizzie said, doubling over with laughter.

Nora came to her rescue. "Never mind him. Let's climb up onto the roof. It's a grand night to watch shooting stars."

"But the trailer's still movin'!" Lizzie protested.

"So?" Nora grinned impishly, then got up and opened the door. "Afraid to fall?"

"Yes!" Lizze exclaimed.

Nora softened. "I'll give you a hand up."

Lizzie watched in amazement as Nora hoisted herself up and out of sight in a few quick moves. She was so strong! Nora reached an arm down from the roof to take Lizzie's hand, and she gripped Nora's hand tight. Below the caravan's single wooden step, the London street was rolling past faster than she liked. Then Nora pulled without warning, and Lizzie was lifted clean off her feet. She managed a sort of flailing scramble up the rear of the caravan, scuffing even more of the paint off as she went.

"See?" Nora said. "Easy."

"Blimey," said Lizzie, settling down on the gently swaying roof. "Good view from up here."

The vast, open arch of the sky was thick with stars, like a daisy meadow. As they watched, a faint streak of light slid silently down the darkness.

"Make a wish," Nora and Lizzie both said instantly. They looked at one another and burst out laughing.

The horse-drawn trailers creaked their slow, steady way through central London. In the streets, the night people were at large. A staggering man, his arm around his friend's shoulders, paused from belting out a song to cheer the passing caravans. A chestnut-seller, tapping the gas from a lamp to roast his wares, called out to anyone who might be listening, "Nuts-oh, pipin' hot! Lovely nuts!"

It was like being in the audience of her very own circus, Lizzie thought from her perch on the trailer. All of London was putting on a show, and she got to watch it.

"We better get back inside, Lizzie," Nora said.

"In a minute," Lizzie told her happily. But then, to her horror, she saw a figure she knew. He staggered a few steps, stopped to prop himself against a lamppost and stare down at his feet, then staggered on. It was Pa, drunker than she'd ever seen him.

"Get down!" Lizzie shoved her friend down flat on the trailer roof.

"Eh?" Nora said.

"He ain't seen us yet," Lizzie whispered.

But he had!

Pa looked up. His eyes went wide, then narrow. "LIZZIE!" he roared.

"Don't look at him!" Lizzie told Nora urgently. "You mustn't look him in the eye. It sets him off!"

"You get down 'ere *now*, girl, do you hear me?" Pa bellowed.

The trailer was passing right by him now. Lizzie didn't want to look down into that horrible twisted face.

"That's your old man?" Nora whispered.

Lizzie nodded.

The trailer shook as Pa's fist slammed the side of it.

"Hey, knock it off!" the driver at the front told him.

Pa sneered. "Who you talkin' to, ya dirty gypsy scoundrel? Eh? C'mon an' take a swing at meh." He hiccupped, and a wave of froth washed out from his mouth and spattered on the pavement.

"Don't look at him," Lizzie pleaded.

Pa began to jog alongside the trailer. "Lizzie!" he howled, as if she'd hurt him. "You've let me down. Me own flesh and blood!"

People were starting to take an interest now, nudging one another and pointing. Lizzie wanted the ground to swallow her up — Pa was shouting even louder than the chestnut-seller was. "I need yeh back! Come home!"

Nora's arm was around Lizzie, hugging her tight. "He'll not take you. Not while I'm here."

Pa stopped, panting heavily, and the trailer began to leave him behind. "I got nuffin' without you, girl! I'm penniless!" He spat the word out, and a lot of spit came with it. "I got debts! I'll end up in the work'ouse . . . all cozza *yoo* . . ."

Then fresh, ugly determination came over Pa's face. His self-pity wasn't working. Anger took its place, and he came charging at Lizzie, his boots pounding the cobblestones. "You selfish little wretch! I'll pull you down, I'll drag you 'ome, I will! By your hair!"

Lizzie clung tightly to Nora, who glared down at Pa. "You will *not*!" Nora yelled down at him. "Get out of here, you old devil!"

Pa spread his arms out wide as he ran. "I'm taking you home . . ."

The next second, he went flying through the air like an acrobat, tripped by a loose stone. His huge chin smashed down on the stones and metallic objects shook out from his pockets and rolled free. He lay with his face in the gutter, groaning, brown mud spattered over his eyes and mouth.

Lizzie stared in disbelief at what had been in Pa's pockets. Gold chains, watches, and coins lay in the dirt. Passing street people descended on the treasures, and Pa was hidden behind a crowd.

"Your da's a thief?" Nora said.

"He always was," Lizzie said, making a sour face. "He's never stolen as much as that before, though. A few silk hankies, the odd watch maybe." *He's gone up in the world since I left*, she thought bitterly.

Nora shook her head. "Pockets full of other people's gold, and he still wants you to pay his debts. The nerve."

Lizzie nodded in agreement, but her thoughts were far away. With her out of the picture, Pa would have been desperate for money. Desperate enough to break into the bigger houses and rob rich people?

Maybe she'd dreamed of the Phantom because, deep down, she already knew who he was — her own flesh and blood. No. It couldn't be. Pa just wasn't clever enough to avoid getting caught. But Lizzie still shuddered at the thought.

"I ain't never going back to him," she told Nora.

"You'll never have to," Nora promised. "You're one of us now."

Lizzie felt close to tears, and not just from the shock of seeing Pa like that. His words had hurt. He'd called her a selfish wretch in front of all those people. For all they knew, *she* was the bad one.

I did the right thing, Lizzie told herself. *He really would have dragged me off by my hair if he'd caught me. Thank goodness for Fitzy taking me in.*

* * *

The circus set up in a wide green park that lay like a blanket in the midst of London's East End. Crowds were already beginning to gather before the tents were even up, and there was a crush to get in on the opening day. The main tent was packed night after night, and the sideshows drew a waterfall of pennies and shillings.

"Always a good stop, the East End," Fitzy told her, surveying the sea of faces. "Your poor hardworking man wants value for money, and that's what we'll give him. I swear it."

Lizzie worked as hard as everyone else. The hard part wasn't seeing people's futures, she now realized. That part was easy. The hard part was telling the client the truth about what she saw. People didn't always like that.

"People don't go to a fortune-teller to be told the truth," Malachy told her. "They want you to tell them that everything's going to be all right."

But Lizzie had made up her mind not to lie, even if it was difficult. An ounce of real help was worth a ton of comforting lies.

June came, bringing blistering heat and even more customers. Lizzie sweltered inside her airless little tent. One especially stifling day, a round-faced man came in. Lizzie already had a headache.

"Now I'm not what you might call a believer," the man said, settling himself in the seat opposite Lizzie. "All this psychic stuff is so much nonsense, if you ask me. But my wife believes it all lock, stock, and barrel, so here I am." He thrust out his hand, daring her to take it.

Lizzie smiled despite the sharp pain building up in her head. She took his hand and the pain suddenly grew, searing through her skull like burning gunpowder.

The pain must have showed on her face. "You needn't bother with the theatrics," the man said smugly.

Right, Lizzie thought. *I'll show you.* She traced her finger down his life line. Visions began to appear, but it was hard to see them clearly through the clouds of pain in her head.

"I can see you walking along a beach, as a little boy—" Lizzie began.

"I was hardly the only small boy to have gone to the seaside," the client interrupted, laughing at his own wit.

"You're crying . . . a crab's nipped your toe, and everyone's laughing."

For a moment the man stopped chuckling and sat still. Then he scoffed. "Happens to lots of children."

Lizzie went on, describing what she saw. Her head was pounding now. The client refused to be impressed, no matter how many scenes Lizzie described. She tried to see clear details, but it just hurt too much.

Suddenly a vision blazed in her mind, clear and bright as the sunrise, cutting through the fog of pain. "I can see a tall house in an alley," she said. "Posh one too. There's a big bronze door knocker in the shape of a lion's head."

She felt the man stiffen.

"You're coming out the door. Big bunch of keys in your hand. Looking left and right."

The man was silent. He seemed lost for words.

Lizzie shuddered. "Something's close, something evil. It's like there's blood in the air."

The customer laughed nervously. "Back to the theatrics."

"It's him!" Lizzie sucked air through her teeth.

"Who?" the man asked.

Lizzie bit her lip. *A man with a mask over his face. Carrying a sack over his shoulder. Creeping ever so quiet and slow. He don't want to be seen.* She strained to see more. She saw a church at the foot of the alley with a golden dragon perched on its tall spire. A voice was calling in the distance. It was the same noise she heard every night. *"Last show, last show . . ."*

Lizzie abruptly dropped the man's hand and took a few deep breaths. "Do you live in a tall house down an alley?"

"No, I don't," said the man.

Lizzie frowned. Maybe her vision had been wrong. Or perhaps she hadn't understood it properly.

"But I *am* looking after a tall house while the owner is away," the man added. "I watch over it during the daytime, then at night I make sure it's all locked up. Now will you tell me what on earth you're getting at?"

"I think you're going to be robbed," Lizzie warned. She deepened her voice so he would take her seriously. "By the Phantom himself!"

The man's cheeks puffed up like a frog's, and he burst out laughing.

"It ain't funny!" Lizzie yelled.

"Oh, that does it!" he laughed. "Wait until I tell my wife! Psychics, indeed." He wiped his eyes. "Dear child, you've put on quite a show for me, but you've pushed it a bit too far."

Lizzie sat there red-cheeked and fuming as the man explained that the police had offered special protection to all houses with valuables in them. The house's owner had asked the local police to keep an eye on his property — and hired him as a watchman for extra protection.

"So the one thing that definitely *won't* happen is a robbery! Not on my watch!" He was pink as a sliced ham from laughing now.

"I know what I saw," Lizzie insisted.

"And by the Phantom, of all people! Tsk! Don't you know that the Phantom has been made up by the newspapers to thrill stupid readers?" He stood up, still laughing, and tossed Lizzie a penny as he left. "You've earned it. What a little storyteller you are!"

"Serve him right if he did get robbed," Lizzie muttered. She sat and stewed for a moment, then made up her mind and sprang out of the tent. She took off running after the man. His life could be in danger. He *had* to listen.

Up ahead, Lizzie spotted the man talking to a police constable. Neither of them had seen her. "Something amusing, sir?" the constable was asking.

"Dark forebodings from a fortune-teller!" said the client. "The Phantom is coming to rob the house I guard!"

The two men laughed together.

"I'd say you've been robbed already, sir, handing over your money to one of them lot," the policeman said. "Don't ever believe a word those circus folk tell you. They're cheats and liars. All of 'em."

Lizzie turned around and walked away before she was seen. The constable's words burned in her ears. "It ain't fair," she whispered. "I'm no liar! I just wanted to help."

Despite the people who swirled around her, Lizzie felt very alone. She knew what she had seen. She might be the only person in the world who knew where the Phantom would strike next!

CHAPTER 10

The rest of the day couldn't go fast enough for Lizzie. There was no chance to get away from the stream of clients, even for a moment. She had to tell someone about the Phantom. Someone who would listen.

Finally, she got her chance. Once the last of the spectators had been ushered out of the main tent, she met Malachy, Hari, and Nora there. Dru and Erin, who was understudying for Collette, cartwheeled through the air high above, cramming in some last-minute trapeze practice. Lizzie almost couldn't bear to look.

Hari studied her. "You've had another vision," he said.

Lizzie stared at him. "How can you tell?"

"You're clenching your right hand. The one you use to do the readings. You did that last time too."

Lizzie felt uneasy. She hadn't known Hari very long, but it was alarming how easily her new friend could read her.

Once Dru and Erin had clambered down the rope ladders, sweaty and breathless from their practice session, everyone gathered in a circle. Malachy sat on top of a hay bale like a king holding court. He nodded for Lizzie to start speaking.

"This is going to sound crazy, but just listen, all right?" Lizzie said. When she had their attention, she continued. "I had a customer today — a man who watches over a posh house. I saw it in the vision. And I saw someone come along with a sack like they was going to rob it." She took a breath. "It was the Phantom."

"You saw the Phantom?" Erin leaned forward, excited. "What's he look like?"

"Nobody knows," Nora said scornfully. "He wears a mask, doesn't he?"

Erin looked to Lizzie. "What'd the mask look like, then?"

"It was horrible," Lizzie said. "Like a ghost, or a skull, sort of. I tried to warn the man, but he laughed in my face!"

Excited chatter broke out. Nobody even questioned the truth of what she'd seen. Lizzie felt buoyed up by their faith in her, as if she'd taken a jump into the unknown, only to be caught by a safety net.

"The question we ought to be asking," Malachy said after the babble had died down a bit, "is why you had this vision in the first place?"

"So I could warn him," Lizzie said immediately.

"But he didn't listen, did he?" Malachy said.

Lizzie frowned. "Lay off! I did my best!"

"I know. But think," Malachy said. "What if *he* wasn't the one who needs to act?"

Lizzie held up her hands. "So who does, then? Me?"

A hush fell upon the gathering. They all looked at one another. Were forces beyond their control setting some great hunt in motion, some adventure beyond anything they'd ever imagined?

"It stands to reason," Malachy said quietly, "that a power that can see the future would have known your client wouldn't listen. So if the vision wasn't meant for him, it must have been meant for you."

"You reckon I've got this . . . this gift of mine so's I can stop crimes happening, don't you?" Lizzie said.

"I honestly do, yes." Malachy jumped down from his perch. "You've already stopped one, haven't you?"

"Aurora," Erin said.

Lizzie remembered Aurora's blood-chilling threats as she was dragged away. She hadn't just stopped a crime, she'd made an enemy. Now Malachy was pushing her to confront the Phantom, who was far more dangerous. All of a sudden, Lizzie felt sick.

"Maybe I should just forget all about it," she said. "It's too risky. I don't *have* to do anything, do I?"

"You can't be serious!" said Nora. "What if you'd just let Aurora rob that man? You think she'd have stopped with him?"

"She'd have kept stealing," Dru agreed. "And when she was finally caught, it wouldn't just be her who got blamed."

"It would've been the whole circus!" said Malachy.

Hari looked up. "If you are the only one who can stop the Phantom, Lizzie, then you have a duty to do so."

"Why does it have to be me, though?" Lizzie complained. "Ain't it the police supposed to stop criminals?" But even as she spoke, Lizzie remembered what the passing officer had said. "I suppose the coppers are a waste of time," she said with a sigh. "At least, that one I saw today was."

"You saw a policeman on the site?" Malachy frowned.

"He spoke to my customer. 'Don't ever believe a word those circus folk tell you,' he said. Called us all cheats and liars."

Eyes rolled and tongues tutted all around the circle.

"*Comme toujours,*" muttered Dru. "The police don't like us, Lizzie. Whenever we come to town, we're the first to be blamed if there's a crime."

"Heard it a thousand times," Nora agreed with a sigh. "Thieving travelers, they think we are."

"A policeman grabbed my ear once," Hari said gloomily. "He warned me not to use my 'Indian rope trick' to climb into windows and steal. I laughed. I told him such tricks are make-believe." Hari pointed at a white scar on his cheek. "He gave me this for talking back to him."

"Safe to say we won't be going to the police," Malachy said. "Sorry, Lizzie. They're always like that where we're concerned."

Lizzie rose to leave. If the police wouldn't help and the adults wouldn't act, then she'd just have to confront the Phantom herself. Once she'd figured out where to start, of course.

"So we'll have to be the ones who investigate." Malachy touched her arm, stopping her in her tracks. "You didn't think we'd let you do this alone, did you?"

Lizzie stared at him. "Seriously? You're all in? Every one of you?"

Nora, Erin, Hari, and Dru all nodded and grinned. Malachy tipped an imaginary hat in Lizzie's direction. "All for one, and one for all."

"Fantastic!" Lizzie cheered. "So . . . um . . . how are we going to catch him, then?"

"The same way we caught Aurora," Hari said. "You recognized the gentleman and his watch, so you were able to act in time. We must look for something similar in this new vision." He sat cross-legged, his eyes closed. Lizzie was sure he was building up a picture in his remarkable mind. "Tell us *everything*," he said. "Take your mind back. Talk us through what you saw. Every detail."

And that is exactly what Lizzie did. She described the tall house, the lion's-head door knocker, the narrow alley, the church with the huge spire, and the flying golden dragon perched on top. Lastly, she told them about the stooped figure of the Phantom, clutching his sack.

Hari asked question after question in a low calm voice, like a hypnotist. "How many windows?"

"Nine or ten."

"Was the sky light or dark?"

"Sort of halfway."

"Was the sack empty or full?"

"Empty."

The questions went on until Lizzie's poor head ached with the effort of remembering. If Hari was growing frustrated, he didn't show it. Somehow, that boy was always calm. Malachy paced back and forth while the others looked on tensely, waiting for the moment of truth.

"Did you hear anything?" Hari finally asked, trying a new tactic.

"Yes!" Lizzie burst out. "A voice, shouting out, 'Last show, last show!'"

"But that's us!" Nora cried, shivering all over. "That's this circus!"

"I've got goose pimples," Erin said with a shudder.

Malachy snapped his fingers. "That tells us when it's going to happen! The callers call the last show at eight o'clock every evening."

"When the sky is half dark and half light," Dru added.

"Now we just need to work out *where* it'll happen," Malachy said. "Let's get to work. We have a crime to stop!"

They all leaped up and began to rush from the tent, except for Hari. "One moment," he said, still cross-legged, holding up a hand.

"Yes?" asked Malachy.

"If we are going to start investigating together, I think we should have a name."

"Brilliant idea!" Erin said. "We should be . . . The Show Tent Irregulars!"

"I don't want to be an Irregular," Lizzie said. "Sounds like someone with an upset stomach."

"Dru Boisset and the Human Oddities?" Dru suggested cheekily. Lizzie cuffed him around the back of the head.

"It needs 'gang' in the title. We should be the something gang," mused Nora.

Hari brightened. "I like that! The Something Gang. It has an air of mystery." He drew a question mark in the sawdust with a finger. "My calling card."

"Too much mystery," said Malachy. "No, I know what we should be. It's obvious. It's staring you all in the face."

They all looked at him, questioningly.

"Well?" Lizzie demanded.

"The Penny Gaff Gang!" Malachy exclaimed.

Lizzie had to agree it was perfect.

CHAPTER 11

The next day was Lizzie's day off. Most of the circus folk went into town when they had free time. The men went to drink and the ladies to shop, but Lizzie had very different plans. It was her versus the Phantom now, even if the Phantom didn't know it yet.

Ever since Malachy had told her not to bother with the police, she'd turned the problem over and over in her mind. Malachy was wrong, she decided. She hadn't even *tried* talking to the police. Yes, her client had laughed with the constable, but maybe she could make a different police officer listen. All she had to do was prove she was serious. Seeing was believing, after all. If she could convince a policeman that she had powers, then they'd have to take her seriously, wouldn't they?

Lizzie ran through the narrow, winding Whitechapel streets, looking for a police station. Alarmed people sidestepped out of her way. A dog tethered outside a pub barked savagely at her.

The more she looked, the more confident she felt. Hadn't the police admitted they were baffled, anyway? They needed any help they could get to catch the Phantom. What did it matter if it came from a circus fortune-teller?

Lizzie finally found what she was looking for on Leman Street. Inside, the police station was gloomy and smelled strongly of soap and writing ink. A desk sergeant with bags under his eyes looked down at her.

"I'd like to help you with an investigation," Lizzie said proudly.

"Get outta here," the sergeant said. "We're not taking on any informants."

Lizzie drew herself up to her full height. "I'm not here to be an informant! I've learned something what could be of importance! Some bloke's going to get robbed unless you stop it."

A second officer entered, mustached and smart in his uniform, carrying two mugs full of tea. He glanced at Lizzie as if she were something a cat had thrown up on the rug. "What's this?" he asked.

"She says she's got *information*," the sergeant said, accepting his tea.

"Has she?" said the officer. "Where'd she come from, then?"

The sergeant's pale gray eyes were on Lizzie, who suddenly found she was having trouble speaking. "Well?"

"I'm with Fitzy's Circus," Lizzie said hesitantly. She was beginning to wish she hadn't come here.

"A circus brat!" The desk sergeant laughed. "Come on then, love. Hand 'em over."

"Hand what over?" Lizzie asked.

"The free tickets, of course." He turned to his fellow officer. "They try this once in a while. Give us free tickets to a show and hope we'll look the other way when one of their lot gets collared."

The mustached policeman blew in his tea to cool it down. "They'll stoop to anything, won't they?"

This wasn't going the way she'd planned at all. "I'm the fortune-teller!" Lizzie yelled. "But I'm not a scammer, I really can see the future!"

The sergeant rolled his eyes. "Pull the other one."

"The Phantom's going to commit another robbery, and you lot need to stop it. If you don't help, then me and my friends are going to have to stop him ourselves!" Lizzie hollered.

"I think this has gone on long enough," the mustached officer said with a nasty edge in his voice. He walked around from behind the desk and loomed over Lizzie, who backed away. He grabbed her ear in a painful pinch. "You and your raggedy little friends should keep your noses out of grown-up business, understand?"

"Ow!" Lizzie hollered. "Stop it! Getcher hands off me!"

The officer dragged her to the door. "You'd better stay on your site from now on, if you know what's good for you. We don't like your sort."

"And if you don't, we've got some nice cells you can come and stay in," the desk sergeant added with a yawn. "If I see any of you circus brats out on the streets playing your tricks, getting in honest people's way, I'll lock you up for begging. Quick as spit."

The policeman dragging her bent down and whispered, "Didn't see *that* coming, did you, fortune-teller?"

Lizzie found herself back on the pavement, rubbing her sore ear and scowling. *Even if they didn't believe me, they didn't have to be so rotten about it!*

She could still hear the desk sergeant talking indoors. "Better see about canceling Overton's leave," he was saying. "When the bloody circus is in town, petty crime goes through the roof. We'll need all hands."

"He won't like it," the other officer replied.

"He can lump it. He's needed. Circus people! They're worse than the gypsies, that lot."

Lizzie marched off down the street, her head full of angry thoughts. *I won't be telling Malachy about this. I know exactly what he'd say — "Didn't I warn you not to bother with the police, Lizzie? They'll lock you up soon as look at you."*

Well, she refused to go back to Malachy and the rest of the Penny Gaff Gang empty-handed. If the police wouldn't help her, she'd help herself. What had Hari said? They knew *when* the robbery would happen. They just needed to know *where*.

Lizzie thought back over what she'd seen in her vision. Tall, narrow houses were everywhere in the East End. So were alleyways. But a church with a golden dragon on the spire? That ought to stand out like a clown at a funeral.

"I'm on the hunt for a golden dragon!" she said to herself, breaking into a run.

Dodging out of the way of ladies with parasols and gentlemen with canes, Lizzie threaded her way through the twisting East End streets. She had to look up often, which meant bumping into people and tripping over cobblestones, but there was no other way to look for a golden dragon over the rooftops.

Lizzie could still see it clearly in her mind. It had a wavy body, like a sea serpent on an old-fashioned map. *Here be dragons*, she thought. Except there weren't any dragons anywhere she looked. She passed ironmongers and pubs and sawdust-floored butcher's shops that reeked in the heat. There were churches, plenty of those. She even passed St. Mary's Chapel with its high white walls. But not one had a golden dragon on the spire.

A nanny went by, pushing a baby. The police had warned Lizzie not to bother anyone in the street. She looked around carefully. No police anywhere in sight.

"Ma'am, 'scuse me?" Lizzie said.

"Hello, petal!" The nanny's face shone like a freckly sun. "Are you lost?"

"I need to find a golden dragon," Lizzie told her. "Have you seen one?"

"I'm terribly sorry, but no. No golden dragons, pixies, or prancing unicorns neither." She giggled. "Good luck!"

"Thanks!" Lizzie shot off down the street, hoping the next face she met would be just as friendly.

But though many of the East End folk were happy to give her the time of day, none of them could point her to a golden dragon. Lizzie was growing uneasy. The more she ran from street to street, the more paranoid she felt. Any moment now, Pa might lurch out from behind a door, full of fury. Madame Aurora could swoop in and grab her.

Or the police might see her. She must have spoken to over a dozen people, Lizzie realized with a sickly feeling. That was surely enough to get her arrested for begging.

I want to go home, Lizzie thought. *Back to my caravan. Forget the Phantom.* But just as she was about to turn around, a sudden tingle in her palms stopped her. It felt like a nudge. "Maybe just one more, then," she whispered to herself. "One more can't hurt."

By now, Lizzie's feet were aching. A woman in a back alley was sweeping dust out of her house in great clouds and squinted at her as she came close. The man lying in the gutter opposite gave her a wave and a drunken grin. His hat was missing its top.

"Golden dragon?" the woman said as if Lizzie had asked for the moon on a stick. "Get on out of here."

"'Ere!" called the drunkard. "I can show yeh! Golden dragons, is it? I see one every day."

"Pink elephants is what he sees," the woman said, slamming the door.

Lizzie helped the drunk to his feet. "Follow me!" he said. He burped, then took off through the streets like a hot air balloon come loose from its tether. Lizzie almost ran into him when he stopped to think.

"Are we there?" Lizzie asked. She couldn't see the spire anywhere.

Deep creases appeared on his brow. Then he held his finger up. "This way!" With a huge stride, he fell over.

Lizzie helped him up again, wishing there weren't so many people watching her. This was taking too long and attracting too much attention. But she continued to follow the drunk from street to street, glancing over her shoulder, wondering how much time she had left.

The drunk repeated "golden dragon, golden dragon" in a singsong voice. Perhaps he was crazy. Perhaps she was wasting her time.

"Hurry up!" Lizzie begged.

"Madam," he told her with great dignity, adjusting his hat, "the game is afoot!" They rounded a corner, and the man suddenly flung his arm out to the side. "Here 'tis! Just like I told yeh!"

Lizzie covered her face with her hand. He was pointing at a pub. The sign over the door showed a yellow dragon with a barbed tail. She read the name aloud. "The Golden Dragon."

"So," the drunk said, grabbing her arm, "have you got a penny for me?"

Lizzie shook him off. His angry yells followed her as she stomped back down the street, picking up speed. *Nothing to do but to go back to the circus. Wasted a whole day.* But at the end of the street, Lizzie stopped dead. The church in front of her looked familiar. Her gaze moved up the elegant stonework, up the long, narrow spire, all the way up to the weathervane at the very top. There it was, glinting in the sunlight — the golden dragon!

Lizzie stopped a passerby. "Please, sir, what church is that?"

"Saint Mary's-le-Bow," the man replied.

Now I can find my way back, Lizzie thought. *I'm not losing this place again!*

The alley had to be close by. Sure enough, she quickly found it, snaking around the back of the church. She felt a thrill as she saw the house, in the plain light of day, exactly as it was in her vision. She wanted to go up and touch it, to prove it was real, but she didn't dare.

"He's coming," Lizzie whispered to herself. "P'raps he don't even know it yet. P'raps he's still choosing the house he wants to rob. But *I* know. And I'll be ready for him!"

★ ★ ★

Once she was back at the circus, though, Lizzie found there was nothing to do but wait. Her friends were busy with their acts. With no work to do and nobody she could talk to, the afternoon passed slow and thick as molasses. She lay in her stifling caravan with the door and window open and listened to the oohs and aahs coming from the show tent.

Finally, the roar of applause told her that the afternoon show was over at last. The whole gang was soon crammed into Lizzie's caravan, eagerly listening to her story.

"We need to come up with a plan," Malachy said, leaning forward from a corner full of shadows. "I say we all get down to the house and find somewhere to hide, then once the Phantom shows his face — well, his mask — then we jump him."

"We can't go," Erin and Nora said together.

Malachy sighed. "Oh, right. You missed it, Lizzie. My dad wasn't happy with the bullwhip routine."

"She messed it up!" Nora jabbed a thumb at her sister. "Came too close."

"By a whisker!" Erin argued.

"Nearly clipped my head off, she did. So now we've *both* got to practice," Nora complained.

"I made it look like I meant to do it!" Erin protested. "Anyway, the audience loved it, so there."

"I cannot come either," Hari said with sad eyes. "My girls are in the show tonight. The elephants need me. If I am not there, they will fret."

Lizzie felt like her chance was slipping away. *This is never going to work. They're all so busy. Why did I even bother?*

Dru stretched like a cat. "I am in the show too, but on last. I will come, so long as I can be back by ten o'clock." It was as if he was talking about going for a picnic. "I think it will be *amusant*."

"You, me, and Lizzie then." Malachy grinned. "Should be enough to catch a Phantom."

Outside, in the humid evening air, they heard a nearby clock strike six. They agreed to meet up in an hour so they could be in Cheapside in plenty of time to set up watch.

"Remember, the cry for the last show is at eight," Malachy told them. "That's when the Phantom arrives, and we spring the trap."

Malachy and Dru went to the tea tent to grab an early dinner, but Lizzie — for once — couldn't face eating a mouthful. Excitement had tied her stomach in a tight knot.

It was time for the hunt to begin, and this time the criminal was the prey.

CHAPTER 12

Lizzie glanced back over her shoulder and caught a final glimpse of the tops of the circus tents before the London streets swallowed them up. Even with Dru walking on one side of her and Malachy hurrying along with his stick on the other, she still felt nervous. It must have shown on her face.

"Would you like to hold my hand?" Dru teased.

"Get off!" Lizzie waved him away. She caught the eye of a stubble-faced man who glared back at her, and she quickly looked away. Was he following them? She put on a burst of speed to leave him behind.

"Hold up," Malachy gasped. His club foot was slowing him down.

"I don't like being out here," Lizzie admitted. "I keep thinking I see . . . people."

"Worried about Aurora?" Malachy said. "She won't lay a finger on you. We won't let her, will we, Dru?"

Dru cracked his knuckles. "I can take her down if I have to. Don't worry."

But Lizzie couldn't shake the cold blanket of fear that had settled over her shoulders. Pa might rough her up a bit, but he needed her alive. But Aurora had promised, "You're dead meat." Whatever else she might have lied about, Lizzie was certain the furious fortune-teller had meant every word of that threat.

"We've got worse than Aurora to deal with if the Phantom shows up," Lizzie said. "He's a nasty piece of work."

"If we're going to get cold feet, then we shouldn't have come!" Malachy snapped. Then, seeing the look of dismay on Lizzie's face, he added, "You're right, though. He did batter that one bloke half to death. We need to be careful."

They turned into Leman Street and passed the police station Lizzie had been thrown out of. An officer was standing outside, but Lizzie didn't recognize him. They kept up a brisk walk until they were far past.

"He might not be so keen to batter us, though, right? After all, we are just kids. . . ." Lizzie's voice trailed off.

Dru snorted. "The Phantom is a criminal. If we get in his way, he'll punish us. So we watch out for one another, *oui*?"

Not another word passed between them as Lizzie led them down street after street, until at last they stood at the end of the alleyway. Lizzie pointed out the tall house with the lion's head knocker, feeling strangely like she was unveiling a monument. "There it is!"

The house stood by itself with narrow alleyways along both sides. Lizzie guessed there was a yard at the back too.

"Looks posh all right," Malachy said, casually leaning against a wall and trying not to look out of place. "Just the Phantom's cup of tea."

"What's the plan?" Lizzie's mouth was dry.

Dru shaded his eyes and looked up. "Climb up the house. Watch from the rooftop until the Phantom goes in. Then we climb down, hold the doors shut, call for help, and . . . *presto!* Caught like a rat in a trap inside the house, yes?"

"Rooftop?" Lizzie said. "Do I look like a flippin' monkey? I can't get up there! Why can't we just hide in the alley?"

"Three children lurking in an alley will attract attention." Dru's eyes flashed with amused pride. "Besides, these houses are as easy to climb as apple trees. You see all the stonework, those ledges, the way the windowsills stick out?"

Lizzie gulped. "It's a bit high up. . . ."

"Trust me," said Dru.

Lizzie could tell he wasn't joking now. She nodded. "All right," she whispered.

"Right," Malachy said. "You two are on the roof. I'll keep lookout from the end of the street and move in once I see the Phantom, because there's no way I'm going up there with you." He turned on his heel and limped down the alleyway, leaning hard on his stick. ". . . be lucky to manage an apple tree with this rotten foot," he muttered.

Dru didn't hesitate. He darted into the alley beside the house, and once he was out of sight, he dug his fingers into the crevices between the corner stones and began to climb. "Do as I do," he told Lizzie, "and don't look down."

"What if I fall?" Lizzie asked nervously.

"I won't let you."

Lizzie took a deep breath. She copied Dru's climb, matching his handholds and footholds. Spiderlike, Dru clambered up and past the first-floor windowsills and edged around to get a grip on a sturdy black drainpipe. He made it look as easy as breathing. There seemed to be a power in his hands and feet that defied gravity.

Lizzie wasn't finding it so easy. There was no safety net here, no rope to catch. Only the hard cobblestones below.

Dru pulled himself up and over the edge of the roof. The gutter looked about to snap under his weight, but it held. Once he was secure, he reached out a hand for Lizzie to take. "Almost there! You are doing well. *Fantastique!*"

Lizzie puffed and gasped as she grabbed the gutter with one hand and clung to Dru with the other. With amazing strength, he lifted her up and over the edge. Lizzie's feet dangled in space for a moment before her weight settled on the warm roof tiles. She clung on, not wanting to move again, ever. *I made it*, she thought, relieved.

They both crouched, breathing hard. Dru grinned at her. "There," he said. "Was that so bad?"

Lizzie glanced down into the alley. Malachy sidestepped into a narrow crevice. From the shadows he gave Lizzie a thumbs-up, and she silently returned it.

The three friends lurked in their hiding places, alert for anything that might happen. Time ticked slowly by. At last there was movement. The round-faced man Lizzie had met before appeared at the front door — the caretaker.

"There he is!" she whispered to Dru. His body pressed against hers as he peered over her shoulder.

Lizzie noticed the huge bunch of keys dangling at the caretaker's wrist. If there were that many locked doors it was no wonder he was confident the house wouldn't be robbed. The man began a careful circuit around the outside of the house. First he checked the iron grilles that protected the lower windows, making sure the locks on each were secure. Then he walked down the side toward the rear of the house, vanishing from sight.

He must be checking the back door, Lizzie thought.

"Get back from the edge!" Dru whispered frantically.

Lizzie leaned back against the sloping roof. She heard footsteps in the side alley below.

"He was checking the windows," Dru explained in a whisper. "If he looks up and sees us — *boum!* All over!"

They waited, hearts pounding, until Lizzie heard the footsteps move away again. She heard the caretaker fasten a lock, then another, and then yet another. She risked a peek, craning her head around to look down. The man looked up at her hiding place, and she whipped her head back again.

A moment passed. A bead of sweat ran down Lizzie's spine. Then she heard the man chuckle to himself. "Just pigeons," he said. He was moving away now, walking down the alley away from them, out of sight. Malachy gave an all clear wave.

The caretaker's heading home, Lizzie thought. *Home to his wife, who believes in all that supernatural nonsense. Funny old world, innit? A week ago, I never believed in none of it myself.*

Lizzie suddenly wondered, with a cold, sick jolt of horror, if the round-faced man would make it home to that wife of his tonight after all. She was sure the Phantom had been carrying a bunch of keys just like his in her vision.

The Phantom must have chosen this house well in advance. And he needed the keys to get inside. So, unless the man was in cahoots with the Phantom, he was going to lose those keys very soon . . . and probably a lot of blood too. Just like that poor man in Spitalfields.

The minute the hour struck eight, Lizzie saw movement from the end of the alley. A man was coming out of a tiny side street, little more than a gap between buildings. She elbowed Dru.

Steadily the figure crept toward the tall house. Every detail of Lizzie's vision was coming to life in front of her. Far off in the distance, the circus callers shouted out, "Last show!" The figure was glancing left and right, cautious as a stalking fox. A sack was slung over his shoulder, he held a black cane in his hand, and his face . . .

The figure looked in their direction. He had no face.

Lizzie was staring right into the ghoulish mask of the Phantom! It looked like a screaming skull, but battered and yellowed with age.

"Can he see us?" she whispered to Dru.

"Let's hope not!" Dru said.

Lizzie stayed still, hardly even daring to breathe, until the Phantom moved on. This was as far as her vision had gone. Whatever happened next was uncharted territory.

The Phantom drew a bunch of keys from a pocket. That didn't make sense. How could he have taken them from the caretaker so quickly? The watchman had left in the other direction.

The Phantom slipped down the little side alley that led around the back of the house, disappearing from view.

"He's heading for the back door." Dru began to clamber across the roof toward the rear. "Follow me. And be careful!"

Lizzie ground her teeth. Climbing on this sloping roof wasn't easy. With every move they made, tiles threatened to break loose.

She and Dru made their way across until they could see down into the backyard. Dru sat straddling the ridge at the top of the roof. "It's easier to balance up here," he offered.

Lizzie didn't fancy it. She peered over the edge and saw the Phantom standing at the back door. He was selecting one key from the bunch, muttering to himself.

Lizzie strained to hear, but she couldn't make out a word. She needed a better view. Maybe if she leaned over a bit more . . . she shifted her weight, and suddenly she was sliding, her foot skidding away as a tile broke loose.

Dru lunged. He caught her dress at the shoulder and grabbed a fistful of fabric. It yanked up painfully under her arm as the tile skittered down the roof. Lizzie prayed it would land in the gutter.

It didn't. It fell and exploded in the alleyway, and a startled yell sounded from below. The Phantom had heard.

Dru stared down at Lizzie, his face twisted in despair. "Get down there!" he hissed. "*Arrêtez-lui!* Stop him! Quick!"

"*How?*" Lizzie asked.

"Down the drainpipe, *vite!*"

Lizzie climbed over the edge and gripped the drainpipe with both hands. She managed a controlled, skidding descent that was a lot faster than the climb up. The Phantom was turning this way and that in the yard. He saw the shattered remains of the roof slate, turned on his heel and ran, heading for the other side passage where Malachy would be standing guard.

"Get him!" Lizzie shrieked at the top of her lungs. She dropped down the last few feet and ran across the yard, past the back door where the keys were still in the lock, and came up behind the Phantom. He was advancing on Malachy, who was bravely standing his ground. The Phantom thwacked the black cane menacingly into his open hand.

"Drop it!" Malachy warned, his voice shaking.

For the first time, Lizzie heard the Phantom's voice. "Move," he growled. "Or I'll split your skull." He spoke in a deep, hoarse whisper. *He's faking it,* Lizzie knew instantly.

"You think a cripple can't fight?" Malachy raised his own walking stick, brandishing it like a war club. "Come on!"

In answer, the Phantom gripped the cane with both hands and raised it above his head. He didn't know Lizzie was there behind him. If she didn't do something, he'd smash Malachy into a broken and bloody pulp. She clenched her fists and got ready to run at him.

Then, to her amazement — and the Phantom's — something snatched the cane right out of his hands. From *above.*

Dru was there, his legs braced between the walls of the passageway, holding him suspended in a chimney-climb. Lizzie looked on in awe as he casually tossed the cane from one hand to the other, his spread legs holding him in place.

"And now," Dru said, "for that mask, eh?" The cane lashed out, striking at the Phantom's face.

It was too much for the Phantom. He ducked out of the way of the striking cane, pushed past Malachy, and ran off in a blind panic.

Dru dropped nimbly to the ground. "He's getting away! Come on!"

The three of them set off in noisy pursuit, Malachy lagging behind. The Phantom was already halfway down the street, running as fast as he could. He tugged the mask off, flung it over his shoulder, and vanished around the corner.

As Lizzie sprinted after him, she heard the clatter of hooves and the sound of carriage wheels beginning to turn. *He must have had his own transportation waiting,* she realized. There was no hope of catching him now. *We were so close! So flaming close!*

Dru reached the mask and grabbed it off the pavement. "We have this much of him," he said with a sigh. "At least, that is — Lizzie!"

"Eh?" she said.

"*Les flics!* The police!"

Lizzie spun around. Four uniformed policemen were sprinting toward them from the other end of the street. *They must've heard all the shouting!* she realized.

"Get him!" Lizzie screamed. "Hurry up! There's still time!"

The policemen charged straight past her. But Lizzie's delight changed to horror as she saw them grab Dru by the arms. He fought, kicking and yelling in French, but they quickly had him on the floor.

"What are you doing?" she howled. "That's not the Phantom!"

"It's him all right," one of the policemen grunted. "Caught him with the mask in his hand!"

"And we'll have that off you too," another one said, wrenching the cane out of Dru's grip. "It's still got blood on the tip, see?"

The next ten minutes passed in a horrible blur. No matter how many times Lizzie and Malachy protested that the wrong person had been arrested, they were ignored. The police found the back door of the house open and retrieved the keys, congratulating themselves on this new piece of evidence.

A crowd was beginning to gather and rumors were flying fast. The Phantom had been caught red-handed. He was a circus acrobat — so obvious! How else had he been able to get into all those houses unseen? And he wasn't even English. Well, you never could trust a foreigner, could you?

In the end, there were so many people filling the alley that Lizzie could no longer see Dru. All she saw were the policemen's helmets moving through the crowds as he was dragged away.

"Where are they taking him?" she screamed.

"Newgate," said Malachy, looking pale and shocked.

Lizzie gasped. Like any Londoner, she knew the name. It was the harshest prison London had ever known.

CHAPTER 13

There were no smiles among the circus folk gathered in the show tent this morning. The Amazon Queen stood there grim-faced; Mario the giant looked as though he hadn't slept; even the clowns looked down at the ground and kicked at the dirt.

Lizzie could hardly bear to look at Dru's family. His father had his arm around Madame Boisset, whose eyes were red eyes from crying. His sister, Collette, hung her head and clasped her hands like a angel.

"As you all know," said Fitzy, "today's rehearsals have been postponed. I've called this meeting to discuss the reason why." A few knowing eyes turned to Lizzie for a moment, then quickly looked away.

Why did that stupid roof tile have to give way? Lizzie thought. She'd never be able to forget the sharp *crash* as it shattered. It was like she'd been trusted with the heart of the whole circus, and she'd smashed it into a million pieces. Nobody had had a kind word for her this morning, except for what was left of the Penny Gaff Gang.

Malachy, who was standing beside his father, gave Lizzie a look that said *it's going to be all right*. But then Collette glared at her with accusing hate, and Lizzie had to close her own eyes.

"I'm afraid the rumors you may have heard are true," Fitzy went on. "Dru Boisset has been arrested and charged with multiple burglaries. They think he's the Phantom."

Murmuring broke out.

"They can't do that!" someone yelled.

"He's only a boy!" cried Anita.

Fitzy gestured for calm. "Please! You will all get the chance to speak."

"Stupid coppers," one of the clowns said, spitting on the ground.

Carefully, without laying blame, Fitzy explained what had happened. He already knew the whole story: Lizzie and Malachy had gone straight to him the night before.

Lizzie winced when he mentioned the vision she'd had. *I wish I didn't have this stupid second sight. All it's brought me is trouble.*

"The police cannot be persuaded that our Dru is not the notorious Phantom," Fitzy finished. "Being in possession of the cane and the mask was enough evidence to convince them of his guilt. The back door of a nearby house was also left open, with the keys in it, and a witness says he saw Dru jumping from roof to roof."

"He is no thief!" Dru's father, Pierre, exploded.

"We know," Fitzy said. "Dru did not steal anything, and nobody is suggesting that he did."

"The papers are doing more than suggesting it!" Mario bellowed to mutters of agreement.

"The papers are not judge and jury, even if they like to think they are," Fitzy said, with frosty calm. "Let's not beat about the bush, my friends. This is a bad turn of events. But it could be a good deal worse. We will make sure Dru gets all the help we can provide, and in the meantime, let's remember we still have a circus to run."

Lizzie felt sick. Dru had gone with her to catch the Phantom. But the papers didn't care about the truth — they just wanted to give the public the story they craved.

"We all know why they've arrested Dru!" It was the Amazon Queen, and she was furious. "The coppers hate us, Fitz. They've always hated us. You've 'eard the names they call us!"

"Of course I've heard!" Fitzy's sudden anger broke out, hushing them all. "You think I haven't been called those names too, ever since I was Malachy's age? 'Circus scum!' 'Thieves and vagabonds!' From the very same people I have to smile and bow to every night!"

There was a hubbub of agreement. Lizzie realized, with some relief, that the circus folk were even angrier with the police than they were with her.

"We all know how it is," Fitz went on. "Whatever crimes they can't solve, they pin on us. Nothing ever sticks, of course, because it doesn't have to. They blame us, we move on to the next town, and the whole business starts over. But this time, they've made something stick. This time they've got a suspect, caught at the scene, and they're going to milk it for all it's worth."

"And whose fault is that?" Dru's father pointed straight at Lizzie. "Who got my boy into this trouble, eh? Who talked him into this stupid game and got him arrested?" He looked around for support. "Who filled his head with talk of visions and told him he could be a hero? Well? Shall I spell it out?"

"Steady, Pierre," said Mario, laying a hand on his shoulder. But Pierre shrugged it off. Everyone was looking right at Lizzie now, and not many of the faces were friendly.

"It should be her in that prison, not him!" Dru's mother sobbed. "And as for your son, Fitz —"

"That's enough!" Fitzy yelled. "It's not Lizzie's fault that Dru's in prison. The coppers are to blame, and you both know it!"

"Dru should never even have been there," Collette said. "If that freak hadn't lured him along, he'd be safe."

"If Dru hadn't been there, Malachy would be dead now," Fitz shot back at her. "Your brother saved my son from being beaten to death. He *is* a hero, so far as I'm concerned!"

Collette had no answer to that.

"Now, tempers are running high, and that's to be expected," Fitzy continued. "But let's not start turning on our own. If we don't stick together, then that lot out there will be only too happy to tear us apart."

A few people yelled, "Hear! Hear!" in response.

Lizzie felt her eyes beginning to brim with tears, not from sadness but from the frustration and guilt boiling up inside her. Whatever Fitzy might say, however grateful he might be to Dru for saving Malachy's life, all this was her doing. She couldn't run away from that.

I'm going to set things right again, so help me, Lizzie thought. *Dru's innocent. I can't let him suffer because of me!*

Zezete noticed that Lizzie was crying and put his arm around her to show he was on her side, then spoke up. "There must be other witnesses, surely. So where are they? Did nobody see the real Phantom flee the scene?"

"We can only hope someone comes forward," said Fitzy. "But even if they do, the police don't want to listen. Dru makes the perfect scapegoat. And the first robbery occurred around about the time we arrived in London, which doesn't help matters."

"So what are you going to do?" Pierre demanded.

Fitzy rolled up his sleeves. "Above all, the show must go on," he said. "Tomorrow, we move to Victoria Park. You all know how important that is. It's our biggest show of the year, and His Lordship the Lord Mayor is coming to open it."

"Always business with you, Fitz," spat Dru's father. "You talk of big shows, of pulling the crowds. But what about my son?"

"Pierre, good publicity is just what we need — and what Dru needs! The more money we raise, the better defense we can pay for in court. If we can get the crowd on our side, or better still impress the Lord Mayor, then we have a real chance of swinging the trial our way. The mayor might even intervene. He could get Dru released on lack of evidence!"

The mayor's a good man, Lizzie thought. *He gave me food and money when I was starving and had nowhere to go, didn't he? If anyone can help Dru, he can. Fitzy's right. I have to win him over.*

"Any questions?" Fitz waited a moment, then clapped briskly. "Very well. Back to work, everyone. Let's get ready for the show of a lifetime."

★ ★ ★

Once the last of the circus folk had left the tent, only the Penny Gaff Gang remained. Lizzie urged them to get on with their practice, but none of them listened.

"This isn't just on you," Malachy assured Lizzie. "We all said we were in this together, remember?"

"We did," said Erin, nodding.

"All for one and one for all," added Nora.

"But, Malachy, your dad said the best help we can give Dru is to put on a good show!" Lizzie paced back and forth, twisting her fingers. "What else can we do for him now?"

"We need to track down the real Phantom," Malachy said.

"That's what got us into this mess!" Lizzie exclaimed.

"And the only way out is to keep going. Dad's right about the show being important, but he knows that's just a gamble. We can't change the public's mind about us just from one show, and we can't rely on the Lord Mayor to plead Dru's case for us."

"He is one of the rich folks, after all," Erin said with a sniff.

"So we deal with this our way." Malachy pulled a folded newspaper out of his pocket and pointed to the headline:

Phantom Trial Set for Tuesday 13th

"We have to do it fast. Dru goes to trial in three days," he said somberly.

Nora stared. "That soon?"

"If they find him guilty," Lizzie said, swallowing hard, "he'll swing, won't he?"

"Yes," Hari said simply, before anyone else could answer. "Robbery is a capital crime. He'll hang for it."

Lizzie felt a sudden pang of guilt. In her caravan, not so long ago, Dru had pleaded with her to read his palm, but she'd refused. But what if she had? Could she have seen the arrest, the imprisonment? Could she have warned him? He would have listened, she knew that for certain. Dru trusted her. She imagined taking his warm open hand in hers, exploring the creases on his palm. If she could see his life line now, would it be long . . . or tragically short?

* * *

Lizzie didn't let herself cry until later, when she was alone in her caravan. "It's not fair!" she whispered to herself, wiping streaming tears away. "Malachy reckons my gift's meant to help people, but all I've done so far is stop rich men from being robbed! What kind of a gift is that? Who cares about rich folks, anyway?"

Lizzie heaved a sob and kicked the wall of the caravan in anger. Then she did it again, wishing she could kick down the walls of Dru's prison cell. She grabbed a flowerpot and smashed it viciously against the wall. That only reminded her of the tile she'd knocked off the roof. It was too much. Her voice rose in a howl of rage and despair. "What's the point of having these special powers if I can't help the people I care about?"

CHAPTER 14

The children at the bathing lake in Victoria Park screamed in delight. "Mummy! Mummy, come and see the ELEPHANTS!"

Lizzie and Hari led Akula and Sashi down into the water, whispering reassuring words of calm while the crowds of children came running up and adults yelled to one another to come and see. Now that the circus had set up here, it was time to get the word out — and nothing attracted attention quite like the elephants.

Akula waded in and dipped her trunk into the water. Some of the more daring boys and girls edged closer, and one even reached out to touch her flank.

"Remember to come and see her this evening!" Lizzie announced. "She'll be performing for the Lord Mayor himself. Only a few tickets left!"

On cue, Sashi blew a glittering spray of water into the air, spattering the squealing children.

It was late afternoon when they led Akula and Sashi back to their enclosure. Excitement was building for the Lord Mayor's arrival. By the look of it, Dru's arrest hadn't hurt business one bit — there were crowds at all the sideshows, and the evening show was sold out. A few people who'd had the foresight to buy up tickets were reselling them at outrageous prices, though not where Fitzy could see them.

That evening, the Lord Mayor finally made his grand entrance. The crush at the park gates was too thick for any of the Penny Gaff Gang to see what was going on. Lizzie ended up perched on Akula's back, shading her eyes to see over the crowd, telling the others what was happening.

"There he is! I see him!" Lizzie said. "He's got a red robe on, with a big gold chain!"

"Is my dad there?" Malachy asked eagerly.

"Yes, I can see his topper. The mayor's shaking his hand. Like they're old pals."

There was a burst of applause from the onlookers. Everybody heard it.

"Who else is there?" Erin asked. "Did Princess Alexandra come?"

"Can't see her," Lizzie replied.

"See, Nora, I told you she wouldn't!" Erin said.

"There's a right crowd of rich folks with the mayor, though. Men in tailcoats with huge beards, mostly. Some bloke in a military coat with loads of medals. And an old woman all done up like a peacock." Lizzie looked again. "They're on the move. They're coming!"

"Get to your places, everyone!" Malachy yelled. "Looks like the mayor wants a tour of the circus. Dad said he might. Give it your best, because Dru's counting on us."

Lizzie sprinted to the fortune-teller's tent and quickly pulled her robes and veil on. Her heart was thumping as she waited to hear the mayor's voice outside the tent. It seemed like only minutes later when she heard the sound of an approaching crowd, and Fitzy's voice ringing out over it. "Now, why don't we begin with a visit to the only genuine clairvoyant to be found in any circus in the land — the Magnificent Lizzie Brown!"

"I happen to be a spiritualist, and I will have you know there are a great many genuine clairvoyants!" she heard a posh woman say, sounding offended.

"Ah, but, madam, they are not to be found in circuses," Fitzy said with smooth good humor. The gentlemen laughed at that.

Oh, lord, I'm the first act he's going to see, Lizzie thought, feeling a little faint. *Please don't let me mess this up.* One of the smaller crystal balls looked dirty. She picked it up and gave it a quick polish.

"I've heard amazing things about this woman," the mayor said. "How on earth did you ever come across her?"

"Fate," said Fitzy. Lizzie knew his eyes would be twinkling. "Your Worship, would you care to experience her talents for yourself?"

"Well, I don't see why not," the mayor replied.

Lizzie heard the sound of tramping feet, very, very close now. She quickly tucked the grubby little crystal ball into her pocket.

"One moment!" said the mayor from right outside. "Ladies, gentlemen, you had better leave me alone for this. After all, if this Magnificent Miss Brown is as good as Fitzgerald claims, she may ferret out some of my secrets! And some of you schemers already have your eye on the mayor's seat, eh, Brundell? Eh, Harpole? You'd love to dig up a bit of dirt on me, wouldn't you? Ha ha! Go on! Be off with you!"

Lizzie heard a great deal of good-natured laughter from the crowd, and then the tent flap move aside. The next thing she knew, the mayor himself was in the tent with her.

"Good heavens," the mayor said, sitting down. "Hello, young lady. I expected someone as ancient as myself."

Lizzie couldn't speak. This task was too important. The words bottlenecked in her throat and wouldn't come out.

"It's the left hand you need, isn't it?" The mayor pulled off his glove a finger at a time and held his hand out, palm up.

"You don't remember me, do you?" Lizzie managed to say. She hadn't meant to say that at all.

The mayor peered at her. "Lift your veil."

So Lizzie did.

The mayor's eyes widened a little, and he smiled. "So, we meet again. Isn't fate a peculiar thing?"

"You were kind to me," Lizzie said. "You gave me money and food, and I didn't even say thank you. I wouldn't be here if it weren't for you, and that's the truth."

"Lizzie," said the mayor, "it was my pleasure to help. We're not so dissimilar, you and I. I think I mentioned that."

"You did," Lizzie replied.

"But I didn't tell you everything. My mother died when I was very young. My father lost his job at the glassworks, because the manager wanted the job for his own son." The mayor paused and looked disgusted with himself. "I'm sorry. I must seem like a self-pitying fool. A ridiculous old man, pouring out the story of my life."

Lizzie tried not to smile. "*I* ought to be telling you your life story! It's meant to be my job."

"I'll make sure to leave a few bits out," the mayor said with a smile. "You can work for your pay! Hard work's how I got to where I am today. I started with nothing."

"I can't charge you, sir. Wouldn't dream of it." Lizzie took his palm in hers. She felt for the first time how gnarled and callused the Lord Mayor's hands were. Not like a gentleman's hands at all.

What an amazing man we have running this city, Lizzie thought. He'd come from the gutter, just like her. But he'd pulled himself up and out.

Lizzie found the life line and gently began to trace it. Blurry images arose in her mind. The mayor as a young man, working in a slaughterhouse, retching at the smell. Lizzie caught a whiff of it, and her stomach heaved. A plump overseer in a top hat cuffed the mayor on his ear and shouted at him to get back to work.

Next she saw the mayor as a young man carrying heavy luggage along a dock. A wealthy man in a fine coat sneered at the mayor as he carried the cases up a ship's gangplank. "Put it down here, you guttersnipe," the rich man barked at him.

The mayor's had a hard life, Lizzie thought.

Without warning, a flash of pain exploded behind her eyes. Lizzie gasped at the suddenness of it, like biting into ice when you have a sore tooth, and almost let go of the mayor's hand, but she knew she had to hold on. Whatever she was about to see was important.

The pain ebbed a little, and bright images began to dance across Lizzie's inner vision, as clear as if she were standing there. She was seeing the evening show. *The future, less than an hour away!*

Erin and Nora went cantering past, standing up in the saddle, broad smiles plastered on both their faces. Rice Pudding Pete smacked another clown around the face with a fish. Collette stepped out onto the high wire. Was Dru there? Had he been released from prison? Lizzie strained to see . . .

Her vision suddenly soared up, past the shocked-looking faces of the audience, and then down into the shadows beyond the stands. Goose bumbs spread over Lizzie's arms as she saw a familiar hunched-over shape edging forward into the light. It seemed to give off evil like a powerful stink. Like the taste of blood in your mouth.

Lizzie knew what she would see when it lifted its head. And she could no more look away than a person trapped in a nightmare can force himself to wake up.

The Phantom looked straight at her. The skull-like mask shone a hideous green under the limelight. Lizzie felt herself drawn into the dark pits of his black eyes, dragged down to be devoured alive.

"Phantom," she said in a hollow voice. All she could think was, *I have to warn the mayor!*

The mayor jerked his hand out of her grip. All the color drained from his face. "Phantom? What do you mean, girl?"

Lizzie shook her head, trying to come back to her senses. "I . . . I seen him! I think he's after you next!"

"But the Phantom was caught. He's in prison." All the friendliness had gone from the mayor's face now. He was looking at her as if she was . . . a freak.

"I seen him before," Lizzie pleaded. "There was this bloke, he came for a reading, and I saw the Phantom coming to rob his house. But the bloke didn't listen, so we stopped the robbery ourselves. You've got to believe me!"

The mayor looked at her curiously. "So the Phantom is still at large, and coming after the Lord Mayor of London? This has to be the strangest fortune ever told."

He'll have me locked in the madhouse for this, Lizzie thought. *With all the other loonies.* But she had to try.

"The Phantom knows you're here tonight, don't he?" Lizzie said desperately. "It's been in all the papers. He's dangerous. And now he knows where to find you!"

For one sweet moment, Lizzie actually thought the mayor might take her seriously. But then he laughed. "Look here, Miss Lizzie Brown. I'm glad I helped you, and you're a plucky little thing. But I'm afraid you've fallen for your own act — hook, line, and sinker! I wish you the best of luck, but you must remember it's only a circus act. Would you do that, for me?"

The mayor stood up and threw the tent curtain open, stopped just outside, and turned around. "And if you do want to earn a living, I'd stop talking about Phantoms and bugaboos if I were you. Tall dark strangers and long journeys by sea, that's what people want."

Fitzy was waiting outside. "How was she, Mayor?"

"Most entertaining!" The mayor laughed. "So, what about this lion of yours, then?"

Lizzie sat there in the dark, shaken. No, she couldn't bear this alone. She had to find Malachy. She hung the *BACK IN FIVE MINUTES* sign outside her tent and ran, still in her mystic robes.

Malachy came straight to the door of his trailer when he heard her hammering on it. "Blimey, Lizzie. Are you all right?"

"No," Lizzie said, feeling her face start to crumple. "No, I'm not all right!"

"Sit down," Malachy said quickly. He fetched her a glass of water. While she sipped it gratefully, shivering in the seat, he found a warm shawl and wrapped it around her shoulders. Once he'd done all he could to make her comfortable, he gently asked, "Now what's wrong?"

"I was doing the mayor's reading, and I saw the Phantom again," Lizzie explained. Some of the water went down the wrong way, and she choked and coughed. Malachy waited patiently until she could speak again. "I think he's going to attack the mayor tonight."

"What exactly did you see?" Malachy asked.

"Just the circus, the acts going out, and the Phantom in the shadows. He was so angry! I could feel it, Mal. He was going to kill someone." Lizzie rubbed her aching forehead. "We have to stop him. I won't let him hurt the mayor. He's a good man. People don't know how good he is."

"But why would the Phantom want to kill the mayor?" Malachy wondered aloud. "Everyone in the city loves him. Unless . . . of course! That's it!"

"What?" Lizzie asked.

"We're all hoping to get the mayor to help out with Dru's trial, remember?" Malachy said. "But the Phantom must want Dru to be found guilty. Dru will be convicted in place of him!"

"So the Phantom must have guessed we'd be counting on the mayor's support to get Dru off," Lizzie said.

Malachy looked grim. "Exactly. And with the rest of the gang in the show, there's only you and me that can stop him."

"We could talk to your dad, get him to cancel the show," Lizzie suggested.

"There's no time for that! It's starting in a few minutes. Tell me more about what you saw, Lizzie. Anything that could help."

Lizzie shrugged. "There's no more to tell. I just saw the Phantom standing there past the crowd, in the dark, near the edge of the tent."

"And the show was already in progress," Malachy mused. "So either he's planning to sneak in once the show's started . . ."

". . . or he's already here," Lizzie finished. "Inside the tent. Just waitin' for the right moment to strike. I have to get to the mayor!"

CHAPTER 15

As Lizzie headed out of Fitzy's caravan with Malachy close behind, she heard a smash and a scream. Anita came running out of her own caravan, pale and shocked. "Someone's chucking stones! My window's broke!"

More stones thumped against the roofs and walls of the trailers. Shouts rang out: "Freaks!" "Thieves!" "Pack up and go somewhere else!"

The Amazon Queen came running from the edge of the site. "There's a mob," she panted. "Throwin' stones at the caravans."

Lizzie badly needed to run and find the mayor. But Anita's face was full of fear, and Lizzie knew she couldn't leave the tiny lady on her own. "Mally, you'd better go and tell Fitzy," she said. "I'll stay here."

The Amazon Queen pointed. "He's on his way already, look. He's brought half the acts with him!"

Lizzie felt bolder as she saw Fitzy storming across the ground toward her. The mayor wasn't with him. Of course not — this wasn't part of the official tour.

Lizzie peered around the caravans to get a look at the mob. There were about fifty people. Instead of going to the gates at the front, they'd crossed the park to the rear of the circus where the trailers were. They stood like a pack of hungry wolves waiting to spring, hurling stones and jeers, but always staying just outside the staked-out perimeter of the circus camp.

"Take this, you thieving scum!" a man yelled as he ran forward. He pitched a huge stone as hard as he could. Lizzie stood paralyzed, staring into the crowd, as it flew through the air and flew straight toward her face.

At the last moment, Malachy tugged her out of its path, and the stone whacked into the dirt. "Lizzie, wake up! What's the matter?"

"He's here," she stammered. "When that bloke ran out, I saw him."

"Saw who?" Malachy leaned in and said in a whisper, "The Phantom?"

Lizzie shook her head. "No." She pointed at the crowd. "My pa."

It was definitely Pa in the midst of the mob, bellowing like an ape, picking up stones and lobbing them along with the rest. Lizzie hid her face. If he noticed her now, he'd take her back for sure, especially with the mob on his side.

Thank goodness, she thought, as Fitzy came striding out to meet the angry crowd. His face bore a showman's grin, but there was a dangerous look in his eyes, and Bungo and Joey walked close behind him, carrying mallets that they swung menacingly.

Fitzy held up his hands, and that alone seemed to quiet the crowd a little. *Nobody could resist the man's charm*, Lizzie thought. But for how long?

"I'm afraid the tickets are sold out!" Fitzy called. "We're about to start. Please go home!"

"We're not here for your show!" someone shouted.

"I see," Fitzy replied. "Then what seems to be the problem?"

The boldest stone-thrower brandished a newspaper at him. "Your boy Dru Boisset, mate! He's the problem! Robbin' the good folk of London!"

"We've all read about him!" someone yelled.

"You're a pack of thievin' lowlifes!" screamed a woman. "We're goin' to come and take back all them things he stole! Just you try an' stop us!"

The mob began to edge forward again, shouting angrily. Lizzie knew they wouldn't find any stolen goods in the caravans. But that wouldn't stop them from helping themselves to whatever they liked.

"Looks like there's going to be a dustup," Fitzy sighed. He took off his top hat and passed it to Malachy. "Keep that safe for me, lad. I'm due to open the show in ten minutes, and I don't want to look like a scruff."

Lizzie could clearly see her father now through the crowd. He was rolling up his sleeves, baring his huge arms. She knew all too well what that meant. *As if knocking me about weren't enough. Now he's going to hit my friends too.*

A fresh stab of cold fear went through Lizzie as she caught a glimpse of who was standing behind him. Tousled hair, pale face — was that Madame Aurora?

"Get 'em!" someone screamed from the back of the mob.

The crowd surged forward and broke through the perimeter, yelling and screaming. Fitzy and the others met their charge head-on and from that moment, it was every man for himself. Circus folk fought with rioters, rolling and tumbling in the dust.

"Come on," Malachy told Lizzie, tugging her arm. "We'd better get out of here."

"Fitzy, where's the mayor?" Lizzie demanded.

"Having a slice of cake in Ma Sullivan's tea tent!" Fitzy shouted. "Tell him I won't be long!"

Lizzie ran, with a quick glance over her shoulder. She saw Mario lift his colossal arms and bellow like a bull, then charge right into the thick of the fighting. He flung rioters this way and that, picking them up off the ground and hurling them off the circus site. A few of the attackers ran away, too terrified of Mario to continue.

* * *

Thoughts raced through Lizzie's head as she headed for Ma Sullivan's tea tent, which was on the far side of the site, far away from the caravans and show tent. If her vision hadn't been wrong, tonight she would meet the Phantom face to face.

Could it be Pa? Lizzie wonderered. The voice she'd heard hadn't sounded like his, but he could have been putting another voice on. He was used to disguising himself when he went out begging. And she'd just seen him moments before, chucking stones with the rest of the mob.

If it wasn't him, then who?

Lizzie thought back to the reading she'd done for the round-faced man, who had been so skeptical. It was a good thing the Phantom hadn't hurt him as she had feared, though somehow he'd taken the keys off him without a fight.

Lizzie frowned. Now she thought about it, she hadn't heard anything about the Phantom robbing a bunch of keys from the caretaker. Surely, if the Phantom had taken the man's keys, he'd have told the police?

A nagging voice at the back of her mind was whispering a question. *Out of all those keys, how did the Phantom know exactly which one to use to let himself in the back door?*

Lizzie gasped out loud. "No," she said to herself. "I don't believe it. It can't have been him!"

What had Hari said? The Phantom wears a mask because he's ashamed. *Ashamed of robbing the property he was meant to be safeguarding, perhaps?* Lizzie thought.

The Lord Mayor had to know! Lizzie put on a fresh burst of speed. *I'll catch you*, she thought. *You think you're so clever, but I know who you are. I'll have the last laugh, just you see!*

Lizzie threw open the flap of the tea tent, but there was nobody inside at all. The long tables were abandoned. Even the trestle table where Ma Sullivan made the tea was empty.

"Hello?" Lizzie called. "Your Lordship? Are you there?"

Nobody answered her. Lizzie began to feel uneasy. Had the mayor left for the show already? She looked around the tea tent for some kind of clue, but there was nothing. Not even crumbs.

"He must have gone in," Lizzie muttered to herself. She looked out across the site and saw the circus folk making their way to the show tent, ready to start. There was Fitzy, top hat back on his head again. They must have beaten back the mob.

Lizzie left the tea tent and headed off across the grass. *Going to have to push through the crowds and reach the Lord Mayor in the audience*, she thought. But just then, she heard something behind her.

Footsteps, hard and fast, like someone running.

Lizzie spun around. A dark shape dodged back into the shadows, vanishing behind two storage tents. She swallowed hard. Of all the people who might wish to do her harm, Lizzie could only think of one who knew their way around a circus campsite well enough to tail her through it, and that was the woman who had been the fortune-teller before her.

Lizzie lifted her mystic robes and took off running. The show tent loomed up ahead of her. Crowds were bustling at the main entrance, and a hubbub of excited conversation reached her ears. Her heart lurched.

They're letting them in already! Don't tell me I'm too late! Lizzie thought frantically. But the sight of the big crowds gave her courage. If she could reach them, she could dive into them. Her pursuer wouldn't be able to follow.

Those running feet were pounding behind her again. Closer, this time. She knew who was coming. Madame Aurora had sworn to get revenge, and now she was going to fulfill that promise. Lizzie put on a burst of speed. She heard her pursuer do the same. It sounded like Aurora was right behind her!

Lizzie looked over her shoulder — and let out a terrified scream.

It wasn't Madame Aurora bearing down on her at all. It was the figure she'd seen in her nightmares. A man in a mask like a screaming skull — not the battered old mask she'd seen before, but brand new and gleaming white.

The mask of the Phantom!

CHAPTER 16

There was only one thing for it. Run!

Lizzie bolted for the safety of the show tent, toward the lights and the crowds of people. Her chest hurt and she gasped for breath as she put on even more speed.

Behind her, she heard the Phantom grunting and panting as he tried to catch up. Ahead, someone was coming out of the crowd, moving toward her. The light behind him cast a long three-legged shadow across the grass. She prayed it was a friend.

Wait — three-legged shadow?

It was Malachy, hobbling toward her on his crutch. He saw who was following, waved frantically, and yelled out a warning. "It's him! The Phantom's here!"

"I know!" Lizzie shrieked. "Get to the mayor!"

Malachy ignored her. He kept coming in her direction, swinging as fast as he could on his crutch and one good leg.

Lizzie glanced over her shoulder. The Phantom was almost upon her now, but he was staggering and winded.

If she was lucky, Malachy might reach her before the Phantom did. Not that two would have much more of a chance than one against him.

Malachy and the Phantom reached Lizzie at the exact same moment. Malachy blocked the Phantom's path, while Lizzie ducked around him.

"Run!" Malachy shouted. "I'll slow him down!"

"You won't," the Phantom snorted in his hoarse voice. Without breaking stride, he thrust an arm into Malachy's chest. The boy fell back and went sprawling on the grass. The Phantom laughed, a gross-sounding chuckle.

This is it, Lizzie thought. *My goose is cooked*. The safety of the show tent was still a hundred paces away. It might as well have been a hundred miles.

But as the Phantom lunged to grab her by the hair, Malachy let out a yell and flung his crutch. It spun through the air and caught the Phantom below the knees. The Phantom stumbled and fell.

"Keep running!" Malachy shouted. "Get to the show tent. There's too many people in there for him to do anything."

Lizzie ran for her life. She was sick with fear at the thought of what the Phantom might do to Malachy, but she couldn't turn around again, not now.

As the Phantom struggled to his feet, he staggered for a moment like a drunken man, then came after her with fresh strength. But now he was limping from where

Malachy's crutch had caught his legs. Grunts of pain came from him every time he moved.

The lights and noise of the show tent loomed closer. *Almost there*, Lizzie told herself. *Come on, girl. You can do it!*

But as she ran, Lizzie realized she couldn't go in through the front after all. There were just too many people to push through. She'd never reach the mayor in time. Lizzie changed direction and ran toward the back of the tent, into the dark shadows where the animal cages were. She dove to the ground and pulled up the edge of the tent, wriggling under the damp canvas fabric, and crawling in. She could smell the moist grass, the sweat from the horses, and the soft warm smell of the whale-oil lanterns. Smells that meant safety.

Lizzie realized she'd come out behind the rows of raised seating, in a dark cluttered space where the unused scenery was kept. The audience were almost all inside, and the show had begun.

"Ladies and gentlemen," Fitzy called, "I welcome you one and all to a night of dazzling entertainment!" Trumpets blared and cymbals clashed. The crowd roared and applauded heartily.

The wall of the tent bulged beside Lizzie, and the canvas flap lifted. The Phantom was fighting his way into the tent. There was only one thing she could do now. Lizzie took as big a breath as she could and screamed at the top of her lungs.

It wasn't enough. The music and the crowd's roaring completely drowned out the sound of her screams. She felt the ground vibrate under her feet. Hoof beats — Nora and Erin must be riding into the ring to start the show.

Lizzie backed further into the shadows, biting her knuckles in pure terror as the Phantom struggled under the lip of the tent and pulled himself to his feet. He glanced around, looking for Lizzie, and quickly found her. He advanced on her, forcing her back up against the tent wall. There was nowhere left to run. As if on cue, the crowd gasped, "Oooh!"

"Don't fight, girl," the Phantom rasped, fighting for breath. "It'll be over a lot quicker that way."

There were so many people in this tent. Any one of them could have saved her from him. But not a single one could hear her. The Phantom lunged at her with both hands.

I'm going to die, Lizzie realized. *Here in the dark, in this overwhelming noise. Nobody's going to find my body until the circus packs up to go.*

Just then, Lizzie glimpsed a rope ladder dangling to one side and decided she wasn't ready to die just yet. She leaped up and caught a rung, pulling herself up out of the Phantom's grasp, and climbing for all she was worth.

The ladder led up the side of the big tent to the very top, where one of the lighting ropes was tied. Those criss-crossed ropes, which were higher than even the high wire, held a line of dangling lanterns that lit the circus from the top down. Every night, someone had to clamber up here to light them. She felt the rope ladder shake and glanced down. The Phantom was following her up — and the whack Malachy had given him with his crutch didn't seem to be slowing him down.

Lizzie kept climbing, hand over hand, until she could see the crowds seated below her. The equestrian show was in full swing, with Nora lashing out with her bullwhip, smacking juggling clubs out of the air as Erin threw them.

Look at me! Lizzie wanted to scream. *I'm here!* But the crowd was howling and stamping with excitement, and the band was playing up a storm. Nobody would hear, even if she fell to her death.

"Keep going!" Lizzie told herself. "You can do this!"

On and on Lizzie climbed. She was perilously high now, almost at the lighting rope. The Phantom was right below her, grunting as he grabbed rung after rung.

Then, suddenly, she was at the top — and there was nowhere left to go. Despair overwhelmed her. As Lizzie looked down at the tiny figures below, the Phantom grabbed her foot! She gripped the rungs tight and kicked wildly, trying to fling him off the ladder. But he was too strong. Now he was pulling her, dragging her down toward him.

Lizzie felt something heavy in her pocket. All at once she remembered the little crystal ball she'd tucked in there.

She flung it as hard as she could, straight for the band, hoping she didn't hurt anyone.

CRASH! went a cymbal, completely out of time. The music faltered.

"STOP!" a voice yelled.

Fitzy? Lizzie hardly dared to hope.

The music fell silent. A chorus of gasps went up from the crowd, and a light flashed across Lizzie's eyes. Someone was shining a bull's-eye lantern up into the high shadows, trying to find them.

"Up there!" Fitz shouted. "Up by the third rope!"

The crowd started murmuring in puzzlement. Was this part of the show? Lizzie had only seconds to act. She filled her lungs and let out an ear-splitting scream.

The light found them. Now there were screams from the audience too. Cries of "Phantom!" rang out all around the ring, and Lizzie saw the circus performers staring up at her, pointing in horror. The Phantom hung frozen in place, the lantern light revealing him clearly.

Lizzie would never get this chance again. She took it.

"Let's see who you really are!" With one deft move, she reached down. The Phantom flung up a hand to stop her, but he was a second too late.

Lizzie tore the mask off his face.

CHAPTER 17

Lizzie clung to the rope ladder, dizzyingly high up, and looked down into the snarling face of . . . the Lord Mayor of London!

"You little fool," the mayor growled. "Do you have any idea what you've done? They've seen my face. They've all seen my face!"

"I—I thought you were . . ." Lizzie trailed off. She couldn't understand what she was seeing. This was all wrong. The Phantom couldn't be the kindly Lord Mayor! Could he?

Lizzie couldn't speak. The Lord Mayor was grabbing her by the throat, one large hand pressed against her, squeezing, squeezing . . .

"Can't let any of them live now," he growled. "They've all seen too much. I'm going to burn this whole place to the ground."

Screams and shouts rang out from down below. Lizzie could hear Fitzy yelling for people to stay calm because the situation was under control, but for once his ringmaster's authority wasn't working. A couple of terrified spectators dashed right across the open circus ring and ran for the exit. One gentleman drew a revolver from his coat pocket and took careful aim.

The Lord Mayor's fingers felt rock-hard, like a marble statue, where they clamped around her neck. Lizzie tried to pry them off, but she couldn't do it with only one hand, and if she let go with the other, she'd fall.

The mayor lowered himself down by one rung, still keeping his tight grip on her neck. Lizzie had no choice but to follow. That was when she realized the mayor was holding her body between himself and the man with the revolver.

"That's right," the mayor hissed. "Keep moving. Nobody will dare take a shot at me if I've got you as a shield."

He needs me alive, Lizzie thought. *I'm going to make it through this.*

Then the mayor leaned close and whispered, "And when I've got out of here, it's curtains for you, my dear." He giggled, a strange high-pitched sound, the laugh of a man whose mind had broken into pieces.

The mayor dragged her down another rung, and Lizzie knew he meant it. She was more terrified than she'd ever been in her life. His grip slackened for an instant, long enough for her to jerk her head back and loosen his grasp on her neck. Words burst out of her. "Why are you doing this?"

The Lord Mayor only grunted, like a drunken man woken from sleep.

"It don't make sense!" Lizzie yelled. "You were so kind to me." *It's like there's a crack right through his mind*, she thought hastily. *If I can keep pounding away at it, he might break.* "You gave me food and money," she said. "And then you nearly killed that bloke in Spitalfields. Why?"

"He got in my way!" the mayor bellowed. His face was bright red now; Lizzie couldn't tell whether it was from the chase or anger. "People shouldn't get in my way. I've been waiting years to get my revenge — and I won't let anyone stop me." He spat the words out in total contempt.

Lizzie knew her only chance was to keep him talking. "Revenge on who? Tell me what you mean —"

"London's a pit! A pit of dung!" The mayor was raving now. Little white dots flecked his face. "You know who the only moral ones are? It's not the police, oh no. It's not the rich folks who hold their leash. They'd step over the likes of me in the street. Maggots. Threw me out. My father too! No, it's the poor. The starving. The ones who've got nothing."

The mayor lifted his hand and closed it across Lizzie's throat again. "This is all *your* fault," he growled. "If you'd shut your mouth like I told you to, you wouldn't have forced me to do this. Just like that stupid man in Spitalfields I had to batter half to death. He interrupted me. It was his fault."

Were those tears in his eyes? Lizzie saw his pupils shrink to tiny dots of sheer madness. She remembered what she'd seen when she'd read his palm. His bitterness over the cruelty he'd suffered as a young man had driven him mad. She looked away, knowing what could happen if you looked an unstable person in the eye. She'd learned that the hard way from Pa.

The mayor's fingers dug painfully into Lizzie's flesh. She wanted to beg him not to hurt her any more, but she knew words wouldn't do any good. She had to let him think he'd won. She let her body go limp, and he took her weight, climbing down another rung.

Through half-open eyes Lizzie watched for something, anything, that could help her to escape. Down at the bottom of the ladder a small crowd had gathered. She recognized Bungo, Joey, Mario, and Fitzy himself. They were looking up at her with grim faces.

"Move aside!" the mayor yelled down to them. "She's dead if you don't. Want me to throw her down? Think you can catch her, do you?"

Then, out of the corner of her eye, Lizzie saw a shimmering white shape. It was all she could do not to stiffen in excitement and give the game away. It was Collette, racing across to the trapeze with Nora and Erin close behind her.

Quickly they scrambled up to the trapeze. Collette took up position on the bar, hanging from it by her knees.

She swung out across the show tent, then swung back and grabbed Nora by the ankles. On the next swing, Nora grabbed Erin by her ankles.

The human chain swayed back and forth, back and forth, until Nora's outstretched arms could almost reach Lizzie. The mayor hadn't noticed — he was too busy shouting threats at Fitzy and his men. But no matter how close Erin swung, she wasn't close enough to grab. There was only one thing to do — Lizzie would have to pull out of the mayor's grasp and jump.

Lizzie glanced down into the terrifying space below, at all the upturned horrified faces. It was so far to fall! There was only one safe place for her to land — the safety net in the middle of the show tent. If she timed it right and Erin caught her, they could swing back over it and let her go.

If . . . Lizzie thought. It was a chance. Her only chance.

Erin's pleading face swung back into view. Her arms reached for Lizzie, but Lizzie froze like a terrified animal. She couldn't move. The mayor was slowly choking the life out of her, and she was just too afraid to fight him.

He's just like Pa, Lizzie thought. *Too strong. You can't win against his kind. They always break you in the end.*

"Come on, Lizzie!" Nora shouted. "You can do this!"

The mayor seemed to snap out of a trance. He suddenly noticed the three girls swinging towards him. A roar of encouragement came from the crowd, cheering Lizzie on.

"No," the mayor gasped. "Got to finish you off. Now."
His grip tightened around her neck, crushing her windpipe.

Lizzie twisted her head around and bit the mayor. She
bit deep and hard like a terrier and kept biting down until
her jaw ached and hot, coppery blood filled her mouth.
The mayor gave a shrill scream and let go of her throat.

Time now seemed to slow down. Lizzie could see Erin
swinging up and toward her. She turned and flung herself
off the rope ladder — out into empty space.

The crowd gasped as one.

Lizzie fell, her arms outstretched and grasping at
nothing. She felt weightless as an angel. The circus lights
rocketed past like shooting stars around her.

In the next second, Erin's hands clasped hers.

No longer falling but swinging, Lizzie hurtled down
past the hundreds of astonished faces, down and down,
faster and faster. Too late, she realized her hands were slick
with sweat, and she was losing her grip.

The net was up ahead, but Lizzie wasn't going to reach
it. One of her hands broke free. She knew she was going to
hit the sawdust-strewn gap and miss the net completely.

Erin tried to snatch her flailing hand back. Their
fingers brushed, but Lizzie couldn't reach. Her arm was in
agony, almost ripped out of its socket, but she held on until
finally her fingers could no longer grip . . . and she let go.

But instead of the back-breaking impact she'd
expected, Lizzie hit something taut and strong that flung

her back up again, then caught her and held her in its safe embrace.

The net. I made it to the net! Lizzie realized.

It was the very edge of the net, she saw as she sat up, dazed. She'd been two feet away from certain death. Erin, Nora, and Collette gracefully tumbled down, making the whole net bounce like a trampoline.

Lizzie looked around, shocked to be still alive, as Fitzy and his men rushed up the rope ladder. With his hostage gone, all the mayor could do was cling to the top and wait to be dragged down. There was nothing terrifying about him now. He looked miserable and pathetic, a broken old man.

Bungo flung him over his back and climbed down the ladder. He carried the mayor in front of the crowd like a trophy.

"Here is your Phantom, ladies and gentlemen!" Fitzy shouted triumphantly. "The real villain, unmasked before your very eyes. Take a good look while you can, because he'll be going away for a long, long time."

CHAPTER 18

"Flippin' heck!" Lizzie exclaimed. She couldn't remember seeing a finer breakfast than the one Erin and Nora brought her — bacon, mushrooms, tomatoes, toast, and some sort of flaky thing like a crescent moon that smelled delicious.

"It's a croissant," explained Nora. "French food."

"Madame Boisset must have took hours to do this!" Lizzie took a bite. It was like tasting the summer sun.

"Actually, Collette made all this for you," Erin said.

Lizzie brushed crumbs away. "I have to go say thanks."

"You'll have to do it later. They've all gone off to fetch Dru from the prison."

Lizzie's eyes widened. "You mean . . ."

"They're letting him go!" Nora squealed.

As they hugged, Malachy and Hari knocked on the door, waving a newspaper. "Read all about it!" Malachy called. "Phantom unmasked!"

"Mayor of London arrested and shamed!" Hari added.

"Get in here with that paper, you two," Erin said. "We all want to hear what they've got to say."

"For once," Nora said with a grin.

They sat together while Malachy read the front-page news aloud to them. Lizzie could hardly believe what she was hearing. With the Lord Mayor in custody, the full story was finally coming out. She could understand the meaning of the strange words he'd hissed at her the night before.

"'Word of the so-called Phantom scandal has already reached as far as New York and Hong Kong,'" Malachy read in a posh voice. "'Lord Mayor Albert Goswin, noted philanthropist and champion of the poor, has been revealed as a hater of the rich. We can now reveal that his habit of robbing the houses of the wealthy stems from his boyhood of desperate poverty. The Phantom's crimes are nothing less than a campaign of revenge against the privileged classes, who the former mayor believes to be responsible for the misery of his youth.'"

Lizzie listened with amazement as Malachy read the story. The mayor was haunted by the fear that one day he might be poor and hungry again. So he punished the rich, stealing their treasures and hiding them away.

"That's why none of the stolen goods were ever found," Hari said. "He wasn't selling them; he was hoarding them."

"But how was he doing it?" Nora asked.

"I'm getting to that," Malachy said. "'Thanks to his position of authority, the former mayor could visit any police station in the city and enjoy unsupervised access to police records. He not only discovered which houses held the most valuable treasures, he was able to steal the keys homeowners had left with the police to ensure their protection.'"

"So *that's* how he got those keys!" Lizzie exclaimed.

"An elegant plan." Hari sounded like he admired it.

"A crazy plan, more like," Malachy said. "He was off his head. The paper thinks so too. "The success of his many robberies over the years convinced the Phantom he had a grand destiny. He fancied himself the true King of London, ruling from his pile of stolen gold, with the people of the city terrified to speak his name. Those who got in his way were swiftly punished, often in the most violent and brutal manner. Rich and poor alike were cut down in his wrath.'"

"Don't I know it," Lizzie said with a shiver. She remembered the Phantom's hands around her neck, squeezing mercilessly. But even though he'd nearly killed her, a small part of her couldn't help feeling sorry for the mayor. She'd seen for herself in Rat's Castle how living in poverty and squalor could drive people insane.

A commotion outside the caravan told them something was happening. They rushed out to see circus folk excitedly dashing from their trailers and heading for the gate.

Lizzie caught sight of a familiar figure riding high on his father's shoulders, and her heart leaped into her mouth. "Dru! It's Dru! He's back!" she shouted.

And they all went running over to meet the Boissets.

★ ★ ★

"Everything they tell you about Newgate? It is true,"
Dru said, accepting a cup of tea from his mother. "Rats the
size of Akula. Stinking filth in all the cells. Lice!"

A party had broken out in Ma Sullivan's tea tent, and
Dru was holding everyone spellbound with stories of
his brief time in prison. "Oh, Lizzie?" he said. "I ran into
someone you know."

"My pa?" Lizzie asked.

Dru grinned. "Madame Aurora. They dragged her
in on my second day — I guess she couldn't give up the
stealing after all."

"She'll be out in three months," Malachy said sourly.

"No, she won't," Dru said. "She's been sentenced to
transportation! *Bon voyage.*'

Lizzie felt relieved. In London, Madame Aurora was a
danger, but in Australia? She'd never threaten Lizzie again.

Fitzy drained his cup of tea. "Well, I hate to break up
the party, but there's work to do. Now that Dru's back, it's
time to move on. We set off for Kensal Green tomorrow."

"Fitzy's is back in business!" Malachy said, flipping one
of his father's hats onto his head in a single throw.

One by one, people began to move away. There
were a hundred jobs to do, and little time for celebrating.

Eventually, only Nora and Lizzie were left. They sat on the caravan roof and watched the circus dismantle itself.

"How's it feel to be a hero?" Nora asked with a smile.

"You tell me." Lizzie shrugged. "If you three hadn't caught me, I'd have been a goner."

"Oh, be serious. What about that gift of yours? All the things Malachy said? Don't you think you've got a destiny?"

"The Phantom thought *he* had a destiny," Lizzie said. "I don't think I like destinies. They drive you mad. My gift, though? That's real enough. I've seen the results."

"So you're going to keep at it, then?" Nora asked. "Solving crimes and helping people and that?"

"Course I am," Lizzie said seriously. "Look. I don't understand *how* I can see this stuff. Don't s'pose I ever will. But I reckon I should use it to do good things. That's simpler than all this destiny rubbish." She drank the last of her tea and looked into the empty cup. "I've never made a difference in the world before. I don't want to stop now. Not ever."

"Never ever?" Nora repeated.

"So long as the visions keep coming, I'll keep using them to try setting things right," Lizzie promised.

Nora leaned her head on her friend's shoulder. "You're a good person. And a good friend."

"Better than my pa, I hope. Maybe that's why I've got the power. To balance out all the bad things Pa does."

They sat in silence for a moment.

"Come on," Nora said. "Let's go see to the horses."

As the girls were walking toward the animal trailers, a shout made Lizzie stop in her tracks.

"Oi! Lizzie Brown! You stop right there!"

Lizzie turned to see her father striding toward her, his sleeves rolled up, his jaw thrust forward. He was stone-cold sober and furious.

"You're not allowed here!" Lizzie yelled.

Pa grabbed her arm in his iron grip. "Shut your yap or I'll shut it for you. You're coming home."

"I won't! You can't make m —" Lizzie started to say. "Ow!"

Pa began to drag her off. "I sure can! You've been earning, you have. Behind my back. That money's mine."

"You're hurting me! Get off!" Lizzie screamed.

Nora took her other arm and pulled, trying to drag Lizzie away from her father. Pa sneered at her, lifted his hand and smacked her. Nora stumbled back, her hand to her cheek, her eyes watering.

"That's what you get!" Pa yelled. "You want more?"

"HITTING GIRLS, ARE YOU?" Pierre Boisset suddenly came storming over, with Fitzy, Mario, and some other circus hands close behind. "BIG MAN, ARE YOU?"

Pa set his hands on his hips. "What're you going to do about it?"

"Let her go!" Pierre warned him.

"Make me!" Pa yelled.

Pierre shrugged. "As you wish." Then, faster than a whip crack, his fist shot out and hit Pa right on his jaw.

Pa staggered like a drunken elephant. Pierre's second punch went into Pa's stomach, doubling him over. Then he hooked a foot behind Pa's ankle and shoved, sending the man sprawling on the grass, coughing and spluttering.

Fitzy held Pierre back before he could do more. "I think he's had enough."

Pa hoisted himself up on his elbows and looked at Fitzy. "You're the boss 'ere, right?"

"I am," Fitzy said.

"That girl's mine. I'm her father."

"So I gathered," Fitzy replied.

"You got no right to keep her!" Pa roared. "She's coming with me!"

"I'm afraid he's right," Fitzy said. "I have no right to keep you here. If you want to go home, just say the word."

Lizzie looked her father right in the eye. "No. I don't want to go home, thanks all the same."

"I know why you want her." Pa coughed. "She's worth money. She's famous now. She ought to be earnin' for me!"

"Her decision is made. You heard her. Good day."

"Now just you wait a minute—" Pa started.

"*Good day*, sir." Fitzy nodded to Mario, who lifted Pa up by the scruff of the neck. The last Lizzie saw of her father, he was being carried across the park, legs kicking in the air.

"Are you sure about this?" Nora asked.

Lizzie hugged her. "More than anything in my life."

★ ★ ★

It was the final show in Victoria Park, and the tent was packed with eager customers. One more special performance, in honor of the Phantom's brave unmasker? Nobody wanted to miss that!

Fitzy had an announcement to make. "Before we move on, it's my pleasure to introduce one last show. Normally I would ask the audience to show their appreciation for the performers, but tonight, both audience and performers want to show their appreciation for one young lady!"

Fitzy bowed to Lizzie where she sat. He gestured for her to stand, so Lizzie rose and took a shy bow, while a storm of applause rained down on her.

A whole show, just for me, Lizzie thought. *I never could have dreamed it.*

The next hour passed like a dream. The Sullivans performed their most daring tricks, finishing off by balancing in an *L* shape on the backs of their huge, golden horses.

Dru walked along the highest of the high wires, juggling as he went. In the hoarse Cockney tones of a newspaper-seller he yelled, "Read all about it! The Magnificent Lizzie Brown bags herself a Phantom!"

Finally the clowns trooped in, arms over one another's shoulders, belting out a song:

"Oh, have you heard the story
They tell all around the town,
Of the girl what caught the Phantom
And pulled his trousers down?
He may have been a menace
But she made him look a clown,
Now he's locked up in the slammer
Thanks to little Lizzie Brown!"

After the clowns came the elephants, with Hari riding Akula at the front. They marched in a full circle, then at his command, knelt down.

With a twinkle in his eye, Fitzy beckoned Lizzie to join them. As the audience gave her a standing ovation, Lizzie stood next to Akula and waved at the crowd. The elephant wrapped her trunk around Lizzie's waist and lifted her onto her back.

As Akula stood up, Lizzie looked out over the cheering crowd. All around the ring, the circus folk — performers and crew alike — stood linking arms smiling at her. Lizzie beamed back, warm in their collective embrace, overjoyed to be part of Fitzy's circus.

This was her family now.

THE MAGNIFICENT LIZZIE BROWN AND THE DEVIL'S HOUND

As the group approached the cemetery, Lizzie kept a careful watch for any telltale glimpse of light that might be the grave robbers. Nothing showed. The moon was hidden behind clouds, and the darkness covered everything.

"We should have brought a light of our own," Lizzie muttered. "A lantern, or a candle. Anything."

"Let your eyes get used to it," Hari said. "Learn to see in the dark. Like a cat."

Dru reached the wall and began to climb. "Better we didn't bring a light."

"How so?" Lizzie asked.

"They won't see us coming." Dru tied the rope around a nearby tree, then threw it over for the others to use. In moments they were cautiously picking their way through the cemetery, alert to any sight or sound that might mean trouble.

"Stay together," Lizzie whispered. She turned to Becky. "We need to check your father's grave first."

"Follow me," Becky replied. "I could take us there with my eyes closed."

When they arrived at the graveside, Lizzie saw what she'd been dreading. The flowers she'd left were nowhere to be seen. "They've been here," she said.

"They robbed his grave?" Becky's voice trembled. She sank to her knees. "How could they?"

"If they're here, we'll catch them," Lizzie promised.

Becky clutched handfuls of freshly dug earth and squeezed them. She rocked back and forth, moaning.

Anyone could see she was in no fit state to take on the grave robbers. "Why don't you wait here," Lizzie said, giving her a quick hug. "We'll find the men who did this."

Becky just nodded weakly and let loose a fresh flood of tears.

I should never have let her come, Lizzie thought. *She's brave, but she ain't in strong enough shape for this.*

Without Becky at their side, Hari, Dru, and Lizzie crept quickly through the cemetery toward where they'd seen the two men before. Dru grabbed Lizzie's arm and silently pointed out a dark shape passing between the trees.

"Is that them?" whispered Hari.

As if in answer, a low and angry growl came from a nearby clutch of bushes. Lizzie barely had time to register that the hound was closer than she'd expected before it ran out, terrifyingly huge against the night sky.

"The Devil's Hound!" Lizzie gasped.

The phantom dog snarled furiously, then ran, and leaped at her . . .